Revolution
SUNDAY

Revolution SUNDAY

A NOVEL

Wendy Guerra

TRANSLATED FROM THE SPANISH BY ACHY OBEJAS

MELVILLE HOUSE
BROOKLYN · LONDON

REVOLUTION SUNDAY

First published by Editorial Anagrama

First Melville House printing: December 2018

Melville House thanks Harbor Mountain Press, publisher Peter Money, and translator Elizabeth Polli, for permission to use Polli's translations of "A Cage Within," "Toy Cage," "Poems In Chinese," "A House Within," and "Playing Hide and Seek"—which appeared in Harbor Mountain Press's full-length poetry volume, *A Cage Within* by Wendy Guerra, 2012.

Melville House Publishing
46 John Street
Brooklyn, NY 11201

and

Suite 2000
16/18 Woodford Rd
London E7 0HA

mhpbooks.com
@melvillehouse

ISBN: 978-1-61219-661-9
ISBN: 9781-61219-690-9 (eBook)

Designed by Betty Lew

Library of Congress Cataloging-in-Publication Data

Names: Guerra, Wendy, 1970- author. | Obejas, Achy, 1956- translator.
Title: Revolution Sunday : a novel / Wendy Guerra ; translated from the
    Spanish by Achy Obejas.
Other titles: Domingo de Revolucion. English
Description: Brooklyn : Melville House, [2018].
Identifiers: LCCN 2018035832 (print) | LCCN 2018043727 (ebook) | ISBN
    9781612196909 (reflow able) | ISBN 9781612196619 (pbk. original)
Classification: LCC PQ7390.G773 (ebook) | LCC PQ7390.G773 D6613 2018 (print)
    | DDC 863/.64--dc23
LC record available at https://lccn.loc.gov/2018035832

Printed in the United States of America

10 9 8 7 6 5 4 3 2 1

For Gabo

Barbara pushed her pale face against the steel bars to look through them. Cars painted green and yellow, freshly shaved men and smiling women passed close by, in a clear parade divided in equal parts by the intersection of the bars on the railing. In the background, the sea.

—DULCE MARÍA LOYNAZ, *JARDÍN*

Revolution
SUNDAY

How can I write all this without getting my pages dirty?

1

I must be the only person in Havana who feels lonely today. I live in this promiscuous, intense, reckless, rambling city where privacy and discretion, silence and secrets, are almost a miracle; a place where light finds you no matter where you hide. Maybe that's why when you feel lonely here, it's because, really, you've been abandoned.

"Don't study so much, but learn," my mother used to say from the depths of my dreams.

I'm one of those people who believes things can always get worse, but this time I was convinced the truly terrible parts had already passed, and nothing worse could happen, or at least that's what I told myself during those months I spent bedridden, delirious, separated from the world and from myself.

One sunny morning, much like all the other mornings of the year I spent in bed, the phone rang. The phone was under a mountain of dirty underwear, fortune cookie boxes, and other leftovers from my confinement. Because the time for condolences was over and there was no one left who cared about me, it didn't ring too often. But now it rang. The last time had been three weeks ago. It had been my friend Armando calling from New York. The pity in his voice was obvious as he sang the words to a well-known guaguancó, "I have no mother, I have no father, I have no one who loves me." He laughed nervously and hung up immediately. Yes, Armando knows I hate condolences, and his sense of humor is greater than my sense of drama. Now, the phone was ringing and ringing, insistently. It rang so much that I had time to crawl out of bed and find it under the heap of trash. Who could it be? There was no family left to deliver bad news, and I'd asked Márgara, our lifelong housekeeper, to stop coming around. I didn't even trust my own shadow anymore, and I didn't want anyone to see me like this. The phone seemed like it wouldn't stop ringing, so I took my time answering. I was beyond being bothered by irritating noises or by any fateful news, apart from that of my own death.

An editor from Catalonia was calling to tell me I had won a big literary prize. They were going to give me fifty thousand euros and, in exchange, they would publish I don't know how many thousands of copies of my book. Did I want to fly to Spain next month to promote the book? Would I have time "before suicide?" the editor quipped, paraphrasing the title of my work. I said yes to everything and then punished myself with a freezing shower to wash away the lingering bitterness inside me. That was the end of the sit-down baths I sometimes took when I bothered to get up. My spine got better on the spot and, even though I had no one to call, lots of people started calling me; journalists and friends of my mother. Cuban authors abroad and plenty of nosy people who simply needed to know what I had done to get something I surely didn't deserve.

I couldn't believe it. At the same time, when I really got to thinking about it, it was everything I had hoped for in life. As a thirtysomething, it fit like a glove. The prize was a stroke of luck that would point the way to the future at a time when the only alternative was to fall into bed and lie there with my eyes open and my mind blank.

What had this year been about? Remembering what happened to my parents, and the strong pressure that came after their deaths.

I closed my eyes to remember the torrent of silver and pain, the dilated explosion that turned the only people who had guided my life into ashes. To close my eyes is to open them to death.

On certain days, I would wonder why I had been saved. Would what was to come next be worth it? Why didn't my parents ever say anything to me? Did they suspect their only daughter? Why did I have to undergo so many police interrogations after their deaths? Who were they, really? There was something more than "Papá" and "Mamá" behind their names.

I rarely got out of bed. The doorbell almost always woke me up. It was them, the secret police. By now I knew it was always them because no one else wanted to get involved in my tragedy. I invited the officers into my room. It smelled bad, yes, but I couldn't be bothered to do anything about it.

The plainclothes officers didn't even look at me; they were obsessed with the idea that I shouldn't speak to anyone, express opinions, or give interviews. Interviews? With whom? For what? No one had contacted me, yet they insisted, demanded silence, asked me to trust them. More silence? Is there anything more silent than this profound mutism? What is left after your voice is nullified by the death of everything you ever had? There's no one here to talk to or with whom to communicate. Sometimes a neighbor knocks on my door to bring me some milk or a plate of food, which I either force myself to swallow or vomit before digesting. But I don't let anyone else in; I'm out of the game. I don't exist.

One of the officers asked me if I recognized my father in my father. What? What was he trying to say? I don't understand. *That* freaked me out. When you're depressed, any abstract idea can send you over the edge. I was living a nightmare, and the officer's light eyes made my head spin. I felt sick and needed to be alone. From that day on I decided I'd never open the door again.

It's been a long year since it happened, and today I'm able to reconstruct events with eyes wide open. How I saw, from inside the car, the dramatic accident at the entrance to Varadero, my parents' bodies pulverized in the air. They were gone forever, and that's all there is to it. How did I survive? I don't know. Miracles happen, and I'm living proof. Why save me, the most useless of all the people in that Russian vehicle?

I shed no tears; I took care of everything and everyone like a robot.

Did I suffer? Am I suffering? Eventually I succumbed. Did that make me a better person? From behind the bars of my two-fisted and indomitable nature, a human being began to emerge. At last I was lying in bed, nauseous and vomiting, suffering from an instability caused by back pain and the depression inherited from my other self, the person who had really written my book of poetry. It was my only book. The one that had won the award. *Before Suicide.*

I danced alone in order to collapse. I spun in circles with a glass of wine in my hand until I felt dizzy, falling to the floor then recovering from my blackout and finding it impossible to fall asleep. I swallowed sleeping pills, opening my mouth like a circus bear eagerly awaiting the sugar cube that rewards its efforts. But my reward was my surrender. Was it so much to ask to disconnect for six hours? That wasn't happening either. I couldn't

even get enough time to escape myself and briefly relieve the
few who were still around to endure my presence.

At dawn, I'd wander the same old streets, where my friends
who'd left Cuba no longer lived. I darted around in fear, rushing to keep up with my pounding heart. During my walks, I'd
often find a public phone and call myself, just to hear my own
voice on the answering machine.

To me, Havana is no longer a capital city. It feels small and
mediocre, and its beauty won't keep it from extinction. A city is
made of its people, and between the ruins and the diaspora, we
are wiping this place out. I don't know the people who live here
anymore; their accents are from the northern coast or the south-
east, they act tribally, in ways that have nothing to do with
the city I discovered as a child. People eat standing up, plate in
hand, or chew and walk on the streets of downtown Havana, La
Lisa, or El Cerro. Foul language and violence have become part
of the landscape, open sewage flows between the sidewalks,
and banging music competes with silence and good manners,
always emerging victorious. Back on the streets, patrolling
its interior routes in search of food or running unavoidable
errands, you end up screaming or mute with rage. Havana starts
to become your enemy; its inhabitants, its inconvenience, the
inability to feel good, it all works against you. This place, once
sublime, now assaults you.

In the midst of all this, I had written some very dramatic poems.
Intentionally or not, they were heartrending. I still wasn't sick;
at that point I could write while pretending to be medicated to

the gills, but my health was that of someone who's only playing a fragile role for a brief period of time.

When you pretend to be mad, you end up going crazy, and when I finished my first book of poems, *Before Suicide*, I really did fall ill. I felt like one of those old, featherless hens, who, after having her neck wrung, still manages to miraculously survive death in the steaming cauldron. Like that, abandoned on the bed, tired and confused, I held out through the nasty tropical winter, postponing bureaucratic tasks like putting my parents' house in my name or opening a bank account with the Cuban pesos they'd left me. I ate whatever the neighbors brought me when they could and I didn't bother eating when no one was around to do me the favor. I stopped checking the mail, I even stopped showering. I became addicted to those mentholated lotions I inherited from my mother and decided to suffer long enough for my body to sort itself out.

No, I don't go to the doctor in Cuba because, ever since I was little, I sensed that my father's laboratory injected poison into people the system considered suspect or problematic. I was convinced someone had tampered with the brakes on my parents' car, making them disappear into the air, taking with them all the lethal secrets they had threatened to reveal if the authorities continued to pressure them. After imagining the hell my parents had gone through at the Scientific Pole, I was no longer willing to go along with their infinite plan.

The day before I declared myself ill, a Monday morning, I walked to the post office, located in the arcades on Infanta, with a recycled yellow envelope in my hand. I wrote the recipient's name on the front, licked the sour gummy edge, and closed it. The sound of the mailbox whispered, "Done." I had sent my first poetry book to a contest in Spain. I had nothing more to gain or lose. I did it because it was my last chance to get out of the hole I was in.

The vomit in the doorways, the smell of fried food, and the voices of the neighbors arguing distracted me. The drumming of the musicians from the *toque de santo* sounded like an omen telling me I couldn't go on much longer. The city I had once loved was gone, along with my friends and everything else.

For a brief moment, after dropping the book in the mailbox, I almost allowed myself to believe I could win the prize. But my neurosis wouldn't let me keep hold of pleasant thoughts for long. Reality took control, destroying any sign of impending triumph, however small or bright it might have been.

And then, despite all my negative thoughts, I won. I won. My poems were able to fend for themselves, and together we were reborn.

As the song says, "Cuando salí de La Habana, de nadie me despedí": When I left Havana, I didn't say goodbye to anyone. At the airport, a man approached me without introducing himself. He was a bureaucrat with the air of a politician. His hands were shaky, he smelled of nicotine, and he had a nervous eye-blinking tic. According to him, the authorities had decided to ignore my book and the award would not be publicized in Cuba. He invited me to consider the possibility of staying out of the country for a while. The comrade, or *compañero*, in the guayabera shirt was an animated, ignorant man who informed me the imperialists were behind my award—an award I had only earned due to a sympathetic marketing ploy based on the unfortunate deaths of my parents. His words gave me several keys to understanding how censorship has worked in this country all these years. He said he was a civil servant. Civil servant? Someone who fell asleep around the time of the Padilla Affair and woke up today? They say those kinds of things don't happen anymore. The truth is, I was only scared for a moment, then I went through security and onto the plane. Madrid quickly wiped away the fearful and parochial thoughts they had tried to put in my head. The narrow-mindedness that imagined "imperialism" behind a poetry prize given to a woman of no significance. Besides, what did my parents have to do with this? They had never even liked my poetry; they didn't understand it. I had nothing to lose. I've never worked for the state, I don't work for any ministry, and it all seems ridiculous. Why would imperialism want to reward my work?

The windows of El Corte Inglés department store and La Casa del Libro were decked out with the cover of *Before Suicide*, whose design featured a renaissance-like image of a hangman's noose next to an unfinished scroll. A clue to the content of the poems inside.

Then came some serious and excellent reviews, dinners with the best and brightest in Spanish literature. Translations, signings, literary events. I went to a few museums, and bought some red boots, a green coat, and white gold earrings resembling a pair I had lost when I was a girl. I filled up three suitcases with books, including some old, illustrated dictionaries.

I needed to write another book. I needed to show my editor there was life before and after suicide. So I applied for three grants in Europe, trying to find a place to write that wasn't Cuba; this seemed like the right thing to do. I was very busy and hardly ever alone. Friends flew in to see me and I traveled to meet them wherever I could find them. So many reunions.

When I returned to Barcelona, I was alone again, and on weekends and holidays I felt like I was dying. I relapsed into insomnia and spent nights walking around my hotel room, surprised by the dawn, planted in a distant bed, a distant life, without knowing which one was mine or where I could find it.

I only returned to Cuba when it became clear I'd have a plane ticket back out in the winter. In Havana, I used part of the prize money to fix up the house. I had enough to restore some old seascapes (oil paintings my mother used to collect), and I sorted out the garden, which had become a total dump. I rearranged the furniture, upholstered the seats, bought sheets and even a water heater so I could shower more often. Was I expecting something to happen? Was I expecting someone to rescue me? No, but my life was beginning to make sense again, just like when I'd had a family and, although now my poetry was the only family I had left, I wanted to make life comfortable again. I wanted comfort in the middle of the heavy solitude nothing could scare away. I wrote at daybreak and, in the afternoons, I tried to walk from Vedado to Quinta Avenida to tire myself out and then be able to fall asleep.

I looked up the numbers of several authors whom I admired and now considered my peers and invited them over for soirées. They would say yes but then stand me up. Who was I to invite them? Just a cheeky stranger whose work many of them hadn't even bothered to read. There wasn't much I could do to socialize. I tried inviting people who, like me, had suffered such silence long ago, but everyone who was still here had been rehabilitated and they didn't want any trouble to intrude on their new and comfortable lives. I tried to find out the times for book launches or readings. When I arrived, no one knew me or wanted to meet me. They didn't talk to me or even offer me a drink.

What could I do? I was living in a country where apparently everyone had agreed to slam the door in my face, but maybe that was just my paranoia. What would my father have said? Was I being neurotic? Was one successful book in Spain not enough to become part of the chosen circle of authors in this country? What is success? I kept trying, becoming a painful nightmare for the local publishers. I took my award-winning book to three publishers and, although I pressed and insisted, I never received a response. Why?

I ate alone in hotels, sometimes with friends of my parents, who usually didn't want to be seen with me. I was an outcast and that feeling grew stronger when I started writing for *El País* whenever I spent time outside Cuba. After that, I was visited several times a month, always by civil servants in guayaberas. They came at lunchtime, just to "shoot the breeze," and during these chats I began to realize I had been elevated to the category of dissident. Why was I now a dissident? It wasn't my poetry, it was my status, the one they themselves had created without even realizing it. They had to put me in a category, regardless of whether it was the right one. They needed to classify me somehow and that's what they did. No one asked if my heart was on the left or the right or what my position was on this long regime. They had already decided it for me. I was a dissident and now they had to "keep an eye on me."

I started buying the coffee I knew they liked. I cooked traditional food on Tuesdays and Thursdays because I knew they'd be sending one of the *compañeros* to me while other officers took care of the rest of the dissidents who, like almost everyone else, I didn't know. In talking with my minders, I found out how much a real dissident made, who brought them their money, and that some of them didn't accept money sent from abroad. I discovered the officers feared or respected some more than others. I walked the streets looking over my shoulder to see if I was being followed, watching out for official-looking cars or shady people dressed in civilian clothes, but I never saw anyone. I detected a suspicious echo on my phone and every time I needed something, someone would turn up at my door selling what I was looking for. A printer, paper, ink, a fountain pen. My personal space became public.

Late one night I decided to go for a walk. I needed to make a choice: insomnia or incarceration, but I couldn't stand both. I started to consider the possibility of finding someone with whom I could share my new poems, the house, and my success, and to relieve the loneliness I had been feeling since before the prize. Yes, that morning, as I stood in front of the Malecón, I swore I would find a lover. In Cuba? Only if I married one of the guys in guayaberas; there was no one else left for me. The salt cracked under my feet like glass dust stepped on by mistake. I stomped on it until I felt like I was walking on waves and, when I was nearly home, I realized just how much salt there was in this city, the salt path being the antechamber from the sea to my house. Havana is a bowl of salt surrounded by water.

When I reached my corner, I checked my father's watch, an old Cuervo y Sobrinos that still worked as well as it did the day it was made. It was too dark to see the time, but from the peace that reigned in the neighborhood, I knew it was well into the wee hours. I looked up and saw shadows at my doorstep. People waiting for me. I couldn't make them out in the darkness; despite my surprise, I found myself thinking I should get a light for the doorway. *A green lamp would look good there,* I mused as I crossed the street, taking note that there were three people at my door. *What do they want?* I wondered as I quickened my step toward them.

"Hello," I said, unable to disguise my unease.

"Hey, hi," they said in unison.

"We were looking for you," said one of the women I didn't know. I noticed it was a man and two women.

"What do you want?"

"Can we come in?" they pleaded as they pointed at the man. I thought it was a bit late.

"What do you want? Who are you looking for?"

"For you," said one of the women, "we're looking for you because—it's about your poems."

My poems? My ego took the bait. "Of course," I said as my key entered the lock and I turned it swiftly, skillfully. Because

I couldn't see anything outside in the dark, I wanted to get inside, into the light, where I could understand things better.

I opened the door and they all exclaimed in awe when I turned on an ochre lamp in the living room. It's true, we had a very special house. One of those old Vedado mansions, the kind passersby marvel at and wonder, *Who owns that? How do they keep it up?* There we were, walking by screens, stepping on kaleidoscopic floor tiles, turning on art nouveau lamps and, above all, breaking the rigorous silence that had filled those rooms for almost two years.

We ended up in the dining room. I sat down to listen to them. It was strange because they kept talking about and pointing to the man as if I should know him, but I didn't. They said he'd read English translations of my poems in the Virgin in-flight magazine, and that he'd fallen in love with three of them, especially the ones from the series *Bob Marley Is Alive and Well in Havana.* It's a text written like a song, which, like reggae, repeats the same phrases and words to dizzying effect, but it's a clearly constructed effect. I don't speak English and so the thin woman who'd originally asked to come in was translating non-stop, which was the only way we could understand each other. The American or English couple took in each of my words, the in-flight magazine still in their hands. I had no idea these poems had been published there, or even translated. I served each of them a glass of rum, and café con leche for myself and the translator. It was getting light out; it wouldn't be long until dawn.

As I drank from my old aluminum cup, the first rays of sun—an amber light—reached through the trellises toward us. Rubén González played on the old record player by request of the strangers, who were all dozing off on cushions by then. That's when, just as I looked at their tangled bodies, I discovered Sting's face. Yes, there was no question, that was him and his wife, Trudie, spread on the floor of my house, drowsy but still aware of the music. Up until that moment, I hadn't recognized them. I finally got it. A chill filled my belly and I sneezed three times, as I'm inclined to do when I'm nervous. I tried to hurry the sip of my café con leche as naturally as possible so I could go the bathroom without waking them. I had to wash my face to regain my composure. I didn't want them to know I'd had no idea who they were or why they'd been so interested in my three sad poems for Bob.

Sting in Cuba. Yes sir, this kind of thing happens: Sting and his wife waking up sluggish on the floor of my home. Anything can happen in Cuba; no need to be surprised. I'd heard many stories about celebrities traveling incognito in Havana, but I'd never imagined Sting could visit my house, where no one wants to keep me company since the death of my parents. I've wound up a stinky orphan, a dissident old maid, a misunderstood and crazy woman who writes poems to be read in-flight. I offered my guests a hot chocolate before they went back to their hotel. Sting was affable, easygoing, thin as a reed, so youthful looking that he seemed more my age than his. His wife kept her distance; she was tough and intense, laughed at everything and laughed alone. Her outlandish Louboutin shoes had disappeared under the couch and it took us a while to find them.

Dressed as if for a yoga class, fresh as a daisy in spite of the rough night, Sting took my face in his hands, squeezed me, and kissed my forehead. He thanked me for my poems and said something else in English I didn't understand. Before kissing me one last time, he mumbled, "Adiós, Cleopatra." I said good-bye, enchanted, and tried to capture the moment with my eyes because I knew I'd never see him again. That wasn't important, though: I may not have ever bought one of his records but he was part of the soundtrack of my generation, that soundtrack that had to contend with a music policy that only allowed one American for every six Latin Americans on the air. Luckily, since he was British, they'd fit him in between mariachis and Argentinian pop. Now all that was left was the scent of almond cream and Chanel, and Rubén accompanying Bob Marley on the piano that bright dawn.

I took a long shower, trying to remember the times I'd heard Sting during my adolescence, the men who'd kissed me as I listened. But none of that had ever happened; no man had kissed me while listening to him. No man ever wanted to kiss me like that before he disappeared forever.

What did he want? To use my texts? I'd said yes before I realized who he was. It's really incredible how literature can soar, travel alone, freely; even when I try to strangle it with my tense and veiny hands, it refuses to condemn me; it flies on its own accord; becomes independent from me; refuses to be silenced; and, if it returns, it's with a different accent.

Still wet from the shower, I threw myself in bed to see if I could finally sleep. When I was right on the edge of going under, the doorbell rang.

Who could be calling so early? It wasn't hard to guess. My *compañeros* would be wanting to know what the lead singer of The Police was doing at my house. I had the same question as I stared at the eyes of the three officers who showed up out of nowhere, thinking I was keeping the best part from them, while, for me, the best part was to remain free to continue writing the texts that brought me surprises like that. My *compañeros* were getting suspicious and I understood it was time for me to play along or I'd wind up in jail for having *exemplary foreigners* like Sting at my house.

The Cuban police don't listen to music and educating them—taking them from his beginnings in The Police through all of his solo projects, and explaining that there's nothing in it that would do harm to Cuba—would require more time than I had to give.

Since I couldn't find anyone who would have anything to do with me, and since I felt watched and empty, I decided to try and salvage what had been snatched from us: the ordinariness of falling in love with people our own age, detoured like a stream, or castrated, as we marched in solidarity with that other silent war.

I made a list of the men who should have been mine, who should have been with me step by step, stage by stage, but were taken from us as if they had been sent to war all at once and then disappeared in that other war because of the strange circumstance of the diaspora. *No one and nothing can keep us from our fate,* I told myself, and I went running toward it, certain I could rescue something of what had been stolen. My next step was to coerce the oracle, or adjust its course.

2

I arrived in Mexico with the idea of drafting an ex-boyfriend who had provided some lovely memories. In order to do so, I called various friends I'd lost during the exodus in the nineties, and at the end of the week we all met up at La Condesa restaurant.

The boy I knew had matured into a man, but he hadn't shed the spirit of adventure he'd had when I first met him. He'd grown up in Cárdenas. The sea came right into his mother's yard, the same sea that washed the halcyon beaches in Varadero. From the time he was a little boy, he'd signed up for whatever water sport class was being offered. He was a natural winner, but what obsessed him was competing. I remember us in a kind of exotic duet: the couple no one could ever quite figure out. His blond hair would waft in the breeze in contrast to my shaved head, my own hair jet black. I didn't play sports. I'd wait for him on the shore as he went out on his kayak and came back to find me facing the clumsy marine scenes I'd painted on cardboard with Russian watercolors. As he conquered the world stroke by stroke, I remained anchored on the shore of our adolescence. Nobody could explain how we understood each other so well. But it was precisely because we let each other be free, until our paths blurred, like my renderings, without our even noticing.

When I found Enzo again, I got an old feeling, my chest began to close in on itself, and when I looked at him I realized he was the same old fighting betta, now with lots of gray hairs and a kind of ashy veil in his eyes. He was, in essence, the same, diving now in a city with no sea.

The friends I'd brought together asked me about Cuba. I tried to explain briefly, in the midst of my agitation, the scenes I'd left behind and from which I needed to get some rest, at least for a few days. But I realized it was important for them to hear my whole testimony, and so I gave it, trying to use images, symbols, to explain what was happening there, narrating what you think is everybody's life. The thing is, each citizen has a personal vision, fragments of a reality other citizens can't see. As I talked about myself, trying to describe a collective situation, I felt a wave of goodwill, because, ultimately, all you can do is tell your sliver of truth. I was the last witness, the last of the beach-goers left in our abandoned city, so I told them about every last minute of my last days to describe what was happening in Cuba. At the end of my story, between tears and kisses, I felt like a hero in the Cuban resistance. None of them could have put up with what we endured every single day. How could they? I could see it in their eyes: They thought those left behind were the residue, the remains, *shell fragments and bad ideas*, the extras in this waste of a film. We were the pack mules heading toward the abyss, burdened with pain, brutality, senseless foolishness, and vulgarity, enduring what little is left of that sixties utopia. Without a doubt, the feeling was an anticipation of the misunderstanding we were yet to have. That's just how I am, an insipid seer who can sense when misfortune is coming, then freezes, unable to do anything about it. My newly recovered friends wouldn't forgive me for staying behind and yet they felt compassion because of all I'd gone through by myself. Why do you stay? Nobody articulated the question but it was there, in the air and the aura of the restaurant. That was obvious. When we were finally left alone, Enzo and I put aside our beginnings and went for a walk, risking Mexico City's danger. After all, could there be a greater danger than all I had told and all I had lived through? What greater danger than having lost them all?

Since what I needed was a warm body, we made love, that's what we did, everywhere: In his building's elevator, he tore my mother's old coat as he went to caress me; in his living room, he undressed me so he could come to me like the great freighter he's always been. That's how I felt him penetrating me, rigid and virile through the moist, warm cove where he'd planted his flag a summer long ago. Here he was, doing battle with the remains of my virginity, from which he'd freed me in beautiful Cárdenas Bay when I was seventeen, right after our school vacation. Enzo destroyed the celibacy I'd taken up in captivity, and with the waters rushing from us both, we sparked a flame between tremors and moans, then surrendered to a final and incredulous sob. How many years has it been since then? Maybe we said goodbye yesterday and all this angst about exile is a fiction that falls apart on contact with flesh? All that time, I lived enthralled by other politics, the politics of the body, caught up in the art of offering it as a singularly free space. I was very much enjoying Enzo. As far as I was concerned, he was perfect, but the shores were calling me away from his body. That's when I understood everything: In our condition, we can't have everything. The shores could wait and our bodies would always feel the swaying, a reminder of our origins, the inner rhythm that follows us and rocks us from infancy. Our habit of lying flat to float on the waves would haunt us forever. When we woke up, we felt sand in the bed, but it was just a feeling, because the shores were distant, as distant as Cuba.

Life with Enzo wasn't exactly life with Enzo. It was collective and communitarian. The shores may have been far but the *cubaneo* was always with us, and constant. We dished about everyone and everything, and lovers were handed off to the next friend who'd then leave with the prior lover's ex. Academic subjects were discussed in the same tone as a recipe for picadillo a la habanera. We didn't buy furniture, or paintings, nothing that would last forever because everyone was supposedly going back to Cuba in ten years (max). For them, the end of the everlasting government was close and they were living its last days.

There was never a lack of moral support. They were kind and generous. They cooked together, accompanied one another on medical appointments, and lived near each other. They called at all hours and planned their vacations at the same time so no one would be left alone in that sober and gray city. Cubavisión Internacional was on all the time in every home to make sure they'd know immediately if anything happened. It was hard to explain that they'd know sooner via CNN Mexico than Cuban TV. How is it possible to forget such essential things about the closed Cuban system in which we grew up and which no one has ever been able to change? To change it would mean to bring the whole system down, and that's one headline Cuban TV will never air, no sir.

They taught college classes, returning under a torrent of rain to their refuge: apartments that smelled of Cuban cigarettes. They wrote articles for the local press about their only subject: Cuba. They would come home exhausted late at night, singing a song by the Trova Santiaguera or an immortal composition by Frank Domínguez. They'd take part in public conversations on panels about Caribbean art, history, and sociology, and never leave Cuba behind. I'd see them come and go from my window. Enzo had a beautiful penthouse with a view in the middle of this ghetto. They'd come and go far away from Cuba, now out of reach in exile, even as it shadowed them everywhere.

One Sunday, Enzo took me to a little market, a discreet little alley in the Zona Rosa. I bought a few books, a silver coffee-maker, and a 1920s purse that looked like the perfect piece Anaïs Nin would have carried around during her New York adolescence. Suddenly, we saw an enormous photograph of Fidel, from when he used to talk to the people in five- and seven-hour stretches. We bought the portrait and brought it to Sunday dinner. My intention was to hang it on the wall, given that our friends couldn't live without him anyway. But that's when the fighting started. They didn't know how to take the joke; the only thing exile had really deprived them of was their ability to laugh at misfortune. To laugh at misfortune meant coming face-to-face with the pain.

Enzo felt abandoned by his friends, who no longer wanted to hang out with me. I had changed him. He didn't want to continue with his political causes and preferred teaching and working as an editor. We planned to move to a beach so we could swim together like before and return to the waters of the past. His friends were unhappy and began using totalitarian tactics: planting doubts, creating divisions with false clues, using rumors to win. There's nothing worse than a communist who's been let down by communism. Who were they and how had they come to be here? If we were to read their real bios, we'd realize how trained they were in these arts. An intellectual exile in dangerous cities without access to the sea can suffocate you. It's not the same as exile in Paris or Barcelona, where you can wander freely. This is a somber exile, seeded with risk and death. How many celebrated Cubans have died here? The list is so long.

I had to put up with it because of Enzo, but I wasn't sure Enzo would put up with it by my side, amid so many conflicting opinions. No matter what, they'd been his family; they'd quelled his fevers; they'd brought him home safely in the wee hours during his nostalgic drunken bouts; they were with him when he found out the horrible news of his father's suicide; they'd toasted when he got his doctorate in history; and they'd never abandoned him on a single Sunday at seven in the evening, when everything seems to cease making sense. And me. Where was I? I'm someone who had died and was now rising through the ashes, the past that has come to unhinge him from the present. As if by magic, suddenly his ex showed up. Horrendous stories about me began to circulate, truths diluted by lies or assumptions to see what kind of effect they'd have on Enzo. While they whispered, I continued working on my book *Dissident Apprentice*, a collection of short essays, written very much in my style, about the Cuba I experienced on a day-today basis. I thought it would clear up my position for my boy-friend's friends and neighbors. Writing was the only thing to do here, because no one could argue with work.

The heat in Mexico City is insufferable. You feel a kind of suffocation at that altitude and the temperature increases the desperation, which keeps you trapped in an unspeakable ardor. I prefer raw winter here; summer doesn't suit this city. We'd go out to the supermarket for groceries and I couldn't help but think about Cuba. I'd been infected with his friends' Cuban illness, which wanted to insert the reality back on the island into this one. At the supermarket, there was everything I'd never had in Cuba, everything we lacked, and everything no one ever needs but is still for sale. I'd look at bathing suits in an attempt to speed up our transfer to the seaside. I'd compile notebooks I'd never fill and bought coconut water so I could taste all my summers in my throat. That's how I endured the heat in Mexico City, and three months later, amid the rains, I had finished my book. The essays laid out a formula, from being a writer who doesn't want to be a dissident, to dissidence itself, all by acci-dent, and described the sociological aspects that might com-pel someone onto such a path. How a simple writer becomes a political animal, that was the subject of my studies. The process undergone by a naïve writer covered in guilt. What to do after a social miscue about a crazy country aimlessly looking for those guilty of its failures. I think, in some way, that became a kind of guide to my readers, a way of being understood by the rest of the world.

I was happy with the results and I think Enzo was enthusi-astic about my new book too. I was ready to read from it for my Cuban neighbors.

But something wasn't right for me in Mexico, in my relationships with Mexicans. I never knew what they were thinking or what they really wanted from us. When I was at a restaurant and looked around, I could see a great gap between them and me. I felt truly distanced from everything in my old life and I held tight to Enzo, trying to understand how he had endured all those years living in a culture so different from ours. Did the Mexicans say how they felt about us? Did they like that we were occupying and invading Mexican space? I don't think so. What would it be like if Cubans had to welcome thousands of Mexicans on the island? And then, when Enzo's friends arrived, I felt a healing proximity, and although they had a certain contempt for this unruly woman who'd come between them, I felt safe in their gestures, their accents, in our similarities, even their intolerance. All of that tied us together, haunted us. Our defects are part of our idiosyncrasies, what we take with us wherever we go.

Finally, the day arrived. Enzo asked his friends to get together, as a birthday wish, so they could listen to selections from my book. We sat in a circle after dinner out on the terrace where we could see the whole neighborhood. Slowly, I explained the basis of my work: a first-person narrative to define the revolutionary context and also to expose myself as part of the experiment, revealing my character and my bad habits, my political ignorance and my fears. To be unmasked was part and parcel of the essay. But as I spelled out my words, I saw myself projected onto a range of experiences, from the little socialist girl to the woman they needed to turn into a spy in order to feel themselves important in the diaspora.

Enzo's friends looked me over as I read, not missing a single detail. They were curious, so I was able to shed the structure and just read the most accessible of the three parts of the book. At midnight, we had drinks and ceased talking about literature.

The idea was to discuss the voice of the essay's narrator. A person who has no interest in being brave but who sees herself forced to confront her fears when she has to defend herself as she contends with the reality inside Cuba. But they thought all that was pathetic and contemptible. Enzo's friends wanted a new hero for Cuba in my essay or, to be frank, in the real world. Wasn't the essay a view from the inside? They wanted a pamphlet to give them hope, something that said: It's possible to be brave and clean without compromise, without duplicity. It's possible that there's a nurturing formula for new leaders in Cuba. That should be possible even in the ravings of a writer like me. They wanted an epic ending, because they were so embedded in the Soviet model even as they rejected it—they denied it and destroyed it in their daily gestures, but that was their foundation: Soviet. Was their Havana my real Havana? This is a very painful and delicate subject. The concept of a hero who doesn't want to be a hero inside Cuba is as real a theme as it is complex. A little bit of fiction in the narrative keeps it from getting too deep. We're in prehistoric times when it comes to genres, and fusing them gives me a great deal of pleasure.

My work was completed and now, on the verge of publication, as I looked at their faces and saw their reactions, I had no doubt: I'd hit a nerve, and that was exactly what I'd wanted to do.

Enzo's friends didn't like my work at all; in fact, it inspired them to do harm. Every sincere act has consequences and, as a result, I spent several days responding to my boyfriend's extensive interrogation. We woke up talking about all that was lost. Depression won out. It was obvious he didn't want to move with me anymore. He killed off his desire to go to the shore; he was suspicious about everything I did. He listened in on my phone conversations. He followed me everywhere. He reread my texts and even opened my emails, both what I sent and what I received.

One afternoon, I went out to buy winter wear. Cold weather had reached the city and all I had were summer clothes—if you can even call my linen and cotton rags clothes. I got out of a legal taxi, the safe kind, and when I went to cross the street to the Palacio de Hierro, two men grabbed me. Without a moment's hesitation, they threw me in the back of a pickup truck like a sack of potatoes. I spent hours and hours riding around the city with those thugs. They'd let me out at an ATM, then at another ATM, then another, until I emptied my checking account. At each stop, they'd threaten to kill me if I moved a muscle to try and escape. They insisted on asking for password after password I didn't know and about Mexican bank matters a Cuban like me couldn't understand. All my credit cards are from Spain and I don't use checks. I have only one password, and the desire to shop, and at that point everything I had to my name had completely vanished. At dawn, they took me to a horrible place: a slaughterhouse for dogs, where they quartered and cremated them. The heap of ashes and the smoke made me falter, the fear of being burned alongside the mountains of hides, bones, and teeth weakened my resolve. When I sat up, I knew I'd fainted, and only being smacked by a pistol and kicked in the back had woken me up. I'd been abandoned on a sidewalk and there I stayed until someone came up to me and asked my phone number and where I lived. I was bleeding, though it felt as if I were washing my hair and the shampoo was running down my back. Somehow, that man found Enzo and we were back in the apartment by daybreak. Frightened, his two Cuban neighbors wouldn't stop interrogating me. They kept asking me if it hadn't been the Cuban Embassy that had kidnapped me. I told them no, that it had been Mexicans, and that they only wanted money. But Enzo had been overcome by suspicion and, when we were alone, he told me nothing like that had ever happened to any of them in that city in more than twenty years.

After what I'd just been through, I thought it was absurd to talk about Cuban foreign policy, about State Security, and about all the foolishness which they wanted to tie to my kidnapping. The ongoing nightmare was feeding Enzo's delirium and his friends' obsession.

"Why do they think the government has anything to do with this?" I asked Enzo. I had a headache so intense I couldn't even close my eyes.

"Because the description of the spy in your book is so impressive, so precise, and nobody can write a diary like that about an experience they haven't lived through."

Where was all this coming from? Didn't it seem a little pretentious? "My God, that's nuts!" I said aloud, trying to sleep unsuccessfully.

I called Barcelona and spoke with my agent and my editor. They were pleased with the first reviews for *Dissident Apprentice*.

I told them I'd be returning to Havana. It was clear Enzo didn't trust me. His neurosis had blinded him and I preferred to think that, if I left, he'd miss me and try to rescue me, pushing back his fear and coming home again, to our first shore. I arranged things with my publisher. We agreed I wouldn't attend any of the launch events in Spain but would deal with the press by phone from Havana; given the book, this was better anyway. I packed my few belongings and said goodbye to our friends, who were suspiciously kind during our final meal together (suspicion had become embedded in everything). Cristina, the one who'd been in Mexico City the longest, asked me to carry a letter for her older sister that no one should read, something about a high Cuban official who was deserting. I was stunned. Why would they ask me to take such a thing if they didn't trust me?

It must have been very urgent, or maybe their suspicion wasn't so great after all and they felt they could use me as a mail courier. Maybe it had been just a passing and silly suspicion, though they'd infected Enzo with it, and he'd become the sailor who fell from grace with the sea. He'd been pulling back so much he'd lost himself among the others. Where was his indomitable spirit? Where was the vehemence with which he had once defended his ideas? Now that he was finally in free territory, I found him more imprisoned than ever.

The Cuba they want needs to be made real, but Mexico City is too far to make it happen between sophisticated cocktails, fights, and past resentments.

They all stayed behind, surrendered at dawn, stretched out on the white couch in the living room, drunk, aged, distant, cold, and sad. The brave long-distance heroes who would save us from socialist anxiety. I grabbed my things and called a cab. I didn't want anyone to see me off. As the sun was coming up and just before I closed the door behind me, I decided not to wake Enzo. I simply left.

At the airport, everything went as expected. The plane left on time, the cabin was jammed with packages, Cubans wandered uneasily up and down the aisle, talking loudly, telling jokes, worried about how much they'd be charged at customs for all they were bringing in. There's practically nothing in Cuba, so we have to import everything. I brought my suitcase and a little briefcase, that's all. I was trying to avoid problems with the authorities, to get through customs inconspicuously and rush home.

Just before disembarking, I remembered I had that letter with me. I thought about hiding it, in case I was searched. I got up to go the bathroom and, as I was about to hide it in my underwear, I decided to open it. Why should I take a risk coming into Cuba with that kind of information without knowing exactly what I was carrying? It was already half open, so I stuck my fingers in the envelope and undid the seal. I sat on the toilet to read its contents.

Pseudowriter:

We knew you'd open the letter. We never trusted you and we became more convinced after you read us selections from your book. That's why you came, to find out about our ideas, our personal Cuba, the new nation we long for. You think you can fool us with your poetic airs but we know you're nothing but a Cuban government agent, a woman who pretends to be what she's not to take advantage of us. That's what you portray in your book: that talent for sniffing around in other people's lives with such naïveté. Our ideas never became clear to you because we were very careful with you from the very beginning.

Please, don't come back. Neither Enzo nor any of us want further contact with you. If you insist, the rumors about you will become headlines, and neither you nor your government needs that.

Go sniff around somewhere else, traitor.

Their signatures were listed below, starting with Enzo's.

I disembarked, leaving the letter in the noisy flush of the toilet, but I don't remember when I touched Cuban soil and if I had everything with me; the commotion was too much. The questions got stuck on the answers, Enzo's nude body, the songs, our happy moments and now this anguish because of a misunderstanding that won't be resolved until we Cubans learn to live together without thinking we're doing each other harm. I felt worse than the day I was kidnapped. I made my way through immigration, where my passport was quickly stamped and a kind official welcomed me. I felt at peace after finally having left that sorry, absurd place. I was home, I told myself as I tried to catch my breath between the cold light of the huge building and the slow spin of the luggage on the carousel. The drug-sniffing dogs walked along side the passengers but I wasn't trying to find my bags. I wasn't doing well. I felt like I was going to faint and fall to the airport's sticky floor. The nurses surrounded me, like they always do, and made me sign a declaration of health that included my home address. Just another kind of control, this time physical. I finally saw my bag drop but when I went to reach for it, a *compañero* in a guayabera took it from me.

"Come, follow me, quietly," he whispered, looking straight at me.

I walked slowly behind him. I didn't know what was worse, to leave the Cubans in Mexico behind or to come face-to-face with the *compañero* in the guayabera. I was losing perspective. Everything was unreal, malevolent.

He left me sitting in a small room for about a half hour without anyone else entering. Finally, a woman came for me.

"What's going on? Why have I been detained?" No one responded. "Why don't you let me go home?" I asked two new officials who were staring at me.

A little later, a man dressed in green showed up with a book in his hands. I didn't recognize the book until they put it in front of me.

"So, dissident apprentice, is it?" the man in green said in a sweet, ironic tone. "Apprentice?"

I asked him for my book. He gave it to me and I had it in my grasp for the first time. The cover was fantastic. A rare joy gave me the strength to ask what it was doing there.

"Does this book of essays really reflect your life?" asked the *compañero* in the guayabera as he neared my chair.

"These are reflections based on certain experiences," I said. "In any case, first and foremost, I am a poet," I said, to explain myself. I was nervous about being there but also happy to have my work printed and in my hands. "Are they going to sell it in Cuba?" I asked.

A heavy silence overtook us.

"Sell it in Cuba?" the man said, laughing heartily now, and looking around for approval from the others in the room.

I interrupted them to explain my question.

"I'm a Cuban writer and all writers want . . ."

"What you've shown us is that you have too much information, and you're a spy, and since you've shown us you've got guts, you're going to work for us. Right, *compañera*?" the official said as he tore out page after page, ripping them up, destroying *Dissident Apprentice*, my first book of essays about Cuba.

3

I'm a model at an exhibition
I live in a human zoo where they medicate and watch us
Reality is curate-able, martial, muddled
And I'm just a spy in the art jungle.

I cross the vast garden. I can feel the wet recently dug dirt on my ankles. I pause to let a marvelous chill run up my body. My black dress seems to shatter when it comes in contact with the night. The full moon poses a threat from infinity and a shiver releases my desire to feel something new. Whatever happens now will be welcomed.

Two fireflies light up my hair, crown my head with brief fluorescent halos. I can see them when I look at my reflection in the windows of this huge house. Everything will be fine, I tell myself. I'm my own nurse, my own psychologist, my own healer. I might be calm, I might be agitated, but I need to take care of myself.

When I'm in Cuba, the landscape, the redolence of overripe mangos, the fury of the ocean testing the limits of the seawall, the frantic desire of men in dark corners drinking rum to calm themselves down takes prominence. Reality is too intense here to feel like a protagonist . . . I disappear . . . My only mission is to observe reality so I can narrate it, which may be why I live as an official reject. However, today, for the first time, I've been invited to "something." It must be irritating to have to put up with a literary person who recounts everything and who, to top it off, gets paid or rewarded for doing so. No person or country, no body or society can keep its privacy around me. To be read—to read me—to be unmasked in a critical version of the story must be insufferable. I go up the brief marble steps, knock on the door, and a uniformed waiter guides me down the ample hallway.

My former housekeeper, Márgara, is back. Could she wear a uniform? I don't think so. All these years of revolutionary orthopedics make it impossible. I'm critical but not authoritarian. We've been disarmed and we don't know how to give orders. I'm completely indoctrinated: social class distinctions are a real taboo for me. Bottom line: Márgara is back. She asked to come back and I said yes, because I can pay her now, and her presence takes me back to the years when my mother would stop talking only to give orders to someone who, otherwise, never responded. Márgara has been and is a shadow. We were together today, alone for the first time without my parents mediating. Making decisions hasn't been a problem because she does everything on her own initiative. She'd left a note on the table with the time, place, and phone number, but I wasn't able to decipher the name of the person who invited me here.

This house could be in the Havana of the 1940s, '50s, '60s, '70s, or '80s; like everything else in this country, it has a timeless quality, an electric patina that reveals its neurotic character. It's been restored, yes, but its veil remains intact.

A grayish-haired, tall European man, accompanied by a beautiful mulatto with yellow eyes, welcomes me. I hold out my hand and thank them for inviting me. They excuse themselves and leave me alone in the middle of this huge hall. It's curious: I seem to know everyone here yet they don't seem to know me. I see faces I've come across a few times at the Cinemateca, the theater, art openings, restaurants I frequented with my parents. Tonight's guests greet me meekly, but with a certain affability. They wave or hug me as they pass but, truth be told, I don't know any of their names. I'm not inspired to sit and chat with any of them; I can't find anyone close or, at least, trustworthy.

Trustworthy: I'm not a trustworthy person either and though I haven't missed a single chapter in this drama, to stay, to watch the whole series while having the chance to leave, to escape it, could be seen as suspicious.

As they interrogate you about other matters, they're thinking, *Why didn't you leave, kid?*

Half the officers assigned to us would give what they don't have to walk the cities I've walked. How many of them would resist the temptation of deserting if they had the same opportunity as all the artists who come and go? I close my eyes and imagine them in Madrid. What would they do then? Would they make a public announcement, desert, or would they simply disappear into the crowd and start from scratch, and forget? Will we be able to forget any of this?

I wander around the living room. A soft current of joy hits my body and surrounds it. Three very well-known writers talk among themselves in a corner in very low voices, trying to be discreet, substituting gestures for words: They pull on Fidel's invisible beard, point to Raúl's stripes, and use their fingers to slant their eyes like his (as if that old sign language couldn't be read). They lean in and chew words in pathetic feminine secrecy. Excited, they talk in gossip mode and look as if they were conspiring. They're the once banned, once prohibited writers, now required reading, winners of national literary awards. They'll go down in history with their incoherence, perhaps as traitors, but only for betraying themselves. Too many years on the same tightrope to keep their balance without panicking.

I live and have always lived in Cuba, but that adherence to a difference of opinion, always between complaints and irreconcilable differences . . . that's suspicious too. How to be here and not give in to the pressures or die trying? Of course, in the eyes of those in exile, I may well be suspicious too. To understand this you have to waste away experiencing it; everything else is an approximation based on past references. The closer you get, the less you understand; the farther away, the more you judge; the more you experience it, the more you suffer; the more you feel it, the less you can let go of the pain. I'm starting to feel a certain attachment to tragedy. I'm adrift.

I look around once more. Who will be the officers assigned to us tonight? Will I know any of them? Then I'd at least have someone to say hello to. Will I be able to say hello to them? Will they pretend they don't know me? Why can't I stop thinking about this?

A soft whisper, a slight whiff of Chanel and reserve rum pushes me toward the couch. A uniformed waiter with white gloves kindly asks me what I wish to drink.

Wish? Wish? Wish? What do I wish?

Again, the possibility of making a choice paralyzes me.

"What do you have?"

"Everything, or almost everything, which isn't the same thing, but almost."

Is this one of those parties where no one dances, where there's much eating and even more talking, and where you find out things you don't want to and shouldn't know? I'm not sure.

Who of all these people put me on the guest list? The host?

I run into two college classmates. They greet me, slightly terrified. I want to hug them but I don't, it's not that big a deal. I say good evening and kiss each one on the cheek; they step away.

Do they know what I do for a living? There's not a book in this entire house. There's not a single bookshelf, just a magazine rack with issues of *Vogue* and *Architectural Digest*. Whose house was this—whose house is this? Is it a rental? It feels like an embassy. Those paintings with the varnished frames—could they be real Lams? Yikes, something isn't right here.

The parties the scientists threw were even more boring. Envy and old resentment would pop out after the second shot of rum. The perks the scientists got in this country were few and far between and they slowly ate at them: your soul for a Chinese TV, your soul for a trip to Europe, your soul for a borrowed house in the Scientific Pole, or your soul for a Lada Riva. Jeez! I'd forgotten about the scientists. My father said few paused to consider what was ethical. The important things were the results. Once they tasted liquor, they let it rip and out came their demons.

Nobody ever punched anybody. The scientists and their parties: dominoes, dark rum, pork rinds, women in white high-heeled shoes and all the men wearing Rolexes. Oh, the scientists.

"Just trust, trust and you'll see it's possible, it's possible to have a life here. Trust: just look at us. We're alive and, in all these years, we haven't lacked anything . . . nothing essential. Nothing, right?" said the ex-minister, a glass of whiskey in each hand, while shooting the word "nothing" right at me, from the depth of his eyes, as if he were launching a dart. "Nothing, right, Cleo?"

Trust is also a theory about the other person's future behavior. An arbitrary, irresponsible commitment. We think we know what's "trustworthy," from our point of view, when, in fact, everything depends on the other person's opinions and actions.

I looked down and took a glass of French champagne. What was I doing at a party with an ex-minister of culture where they served pink Moët? He showed up out of nowhere. Does he know me? Who or what brought us both here? I stared at him to try to greet him but he shifted his gaze. Here's something true of this country's official leadership: their way of dressing, their insistence on being or seeming humble, on turning their backs to market forces, on need, with the only option being to wear whatever's available, because they're also lacking the resources to buy the appropriate wardrobe but, also, because this way they underscore their disdain for fashion and the way they love not being a part of it. They walk into embassies and receptions proud of their safari jackets, their guayaberas, their plaid shirts, their classic carpenter pants. None of it looks good on them but it brings them peace of mind, they think they go unnoticed, except at parties like this one. I've always thought that this non-style germinates an unquestionable condition: contempt for beauty, for the value of the moment and its inspiring and symbolic aesthetic and historic changes. That disdain, that glorified and perennial collective olive-green posture, registers "macho" and uniformity, it personifies that attitude of sameness that absorbs us into the masses, where our ideas about guerrilla life are fortified, and the slightest pang of individuality, tenderness, personal touch, or wink toward visual independence is crushed.

Power doesn't need to show off its luxury. What's truly luxurious is to own a country and strip it of all style, and also of the possibility of choosing its own emotional aesthetic. For more than five decades, scarcity marked our bodies and we learned to dress in practically nothing, only what we could inherit, recycle, or salvage from the wreck.

Fashion here has been precisely that—to live with our backs to fashion. It's politically correct to be humble. It's not advisable to wear anything expensive, or well designed, extravagant, out of the ordinary, unique, not mass produced, or that in any way reminds us there are other ways of going through life. It's not advisable to be original.

I look at my clothes: They're beautiful but common, thoughtlessly put together, too relaxed, I'd say, and designed by . . . I don't know. I never learned how to dress myself, my parents weren't interested in clothing. All this means I've never discovered my own style. I have no personal aesthetic: I'm not a rocker, nor sophisticated, nor a romantic . . . I realize what I'm wearing is a disguise, something to help me get lost in the crowd. My clothes take care of me, guard me; they're my second skin. In other words, when it comes to fashion, I'm as handicapped as the next person.

I so want to spend time with someone, especially someone to whom I don't have to explain what's happened to me in the last two years.

Being read, honored, translated into several languages doesn't matter if you're not recognized in your own country, if you can't find your original readers, if you can't share your work with your own people.

I'm a woman who writes and talks to herself and travels the world like that, who's read in that other world, which, here, we pretend doesn't exist. I just want to be heard. Not as a writer, not as an intellectual. I just want to have a conversation with some-one who won't be terrified when I draw near. Is there anyone I can trust?

"Let's go the pool, please," the waiter said attentively as he handed me another glass of champagne, this one in a fine, ele-gant and iced Baccarat crystal. A light murmur circled the room and I heard, in perfect French, *"Bal masqué!"*

They opened the great big mirrored picture windows, and heat and light hit the room. The magic unfurled in Isaac Del-gado's voice as he was accompanied by his group. I couldn't believe it. The pool offered a nautical reflection that made it seem as if the patio was undulating. The lights colored the trees in violet, blue, and magenta tones. The mangos appeared to be splattered with a kind of bright rosacea and the avocados looked like illuminated eggplants.

A legion of waiters began distributing Venetian masks. I thought a bit of flirtation might be fun and I chose a hand-held one, so I could be recognized in case I ran into anyone I knew.

But why should I be recognized? That would make me believe in the construction of this artificial silence. Cat eyes, red and jade tulle, a little black velvet, and a certain pearl on my right cheek like a black tear. I want to be discovered and this mask will not ruin it for me, no, sir.

Your feet follow the rhythm to the music along the slippery moss by the pool and the soft Japanese grass. "*Tengo un equilibrio, con dos, con dos mujeres,*" Isaac sings during a medley of his greatest hits. He's come back to live on the island and it feels like he's never left . . . what a feeling! What giddiness! People have lost the habit of dancing in couples but this rueda de casino dancing circle in the patio allows me to try out each of the dancers, and I love that. I haven't spoken with anyone but now I'm dancing with everyone. That's Cuba. When it comes to moving your body, to touching and being touched, then all suspicion is set aside. It's because in the last few years the body has been the only truly free space we Cubans have had. I can't see their faces, I don't know who they are, but I can guess their ages by their stepping style, by the way they hold me, throw me out, and then bring me back right as I hit the point of breaking free. I float from hand to hand, loose and light, independent and sovereign, until I'm firmly trapped by a dancer from the old guard who holds on to my waist, marking time, turning, making me his to the two/four beat.

A group of fifteen or twenty people, their masks very well

fitted, crosses the garden. The ex-minister greets them warmly, while the waiters make way for them at the VIP area next to the orchestra, now on a break to allow the main masked man to speak. There's no doubt now—he's the owner of this beautiful 1940s house in the very heart of Vedado.

"Hello everyone," he says in an odd accent. Feedback screeches uncomfortably, interrupting the foreigner's speech. His accent is hard to decipher. French? Belgium? After a few technical adjustments, he continues, "Yes, hello again. We're inaugurating our house in Havana tonight and we want to thank the authorities, because they've helped us rescue this palace from the last century. Abel, my Cuban husband, and I are sure this will be a gathering place for culture and delight for all our friends who love art and a good meal. Tonight we've invited all our collaborators from when I was ambassador, as well as all the people we feel are great international figures of Cuban culture. We don't know many of you, but we'll stop by and get to know you as the evening progresses. There'll be introductions, reunions, then dinner, and, of course, more and more music until midnight. It's a real pleasure to have you here. Welcome home. *¡Salud!*" says the ex-ambassador from . . . ? Then he makes room for his husband, Abel, who speaks by putting his mouth right on the microphone.

"Let's rip it up, people, cuz the world is gonna end! And thanks for coming!" The beautiful mulatto glances somewhat anxiously at the ex-ambassador and hesitates before continuing, "Oh, please, don't do this to me, baby, you know I don't like speeches—that's your thing. People . . . never mind, thank you and . . . get to it, Isaac!" he says, snapping his fingers and letting the musicians know their break is over.

The orchestra starts playing just in time to accompany my third glass of champagne.

"Lluvia Martines, pleased to meet you," says a woman with a Mexican accent as she tries to fix the mask on her glasses while balancing herself on the soft grass and holding her little black silk purse and an unsteady glass of champagne. I hold out my hand and she leans on me to kiss my cheek.

"May I help you with your mask?"

"Yes, please."

After I fix her mask and attempt to introduce myself, Lluvia interrupts me to say she is an editor and knows who I am.

"You're the poet."

"Yes, Cleo. It's a pleasure to meet you."

"I thought they didn't publish you here, that they ignored you."

"That's right," I say as I look around.

"So then what are you doing at this party with ex-ministers and official writers?"

"Well, actually, I don't know. I think it's been a great misunderstanding on my part, and a mistake on theirs as well to invite me."

"Well, then, let's toast to that misunderstanding. Thanks to that, we've met. I saw your face in Paris, on the huge banners at the Rodin Museum for that exhibition on contemporary art and poetry. Lovely photo, and lovely verse. Let's see if I remember . . . *They can't expel me from the island that is me myself.*"

"Well, yes, what a memory. The text reads: *They can't expel me from the island that is me.*"

"Wonderful. You know, I was thinking about you today because I want . . . my cousin, Gerónimo Martines, is arriving in a few days . . ."

"The actor?"

Just then the ex-minister conveniently interrupts our chat.

"Lluvia, I want to introduce you to two great poets . . ."

"Oh, I'll be with you in a minute. It's just that I was trying to tell Cleo about my project . . . because I think, ex-minister, that Cleo is the . . ."

"Excuse me, Cleo. This way, Lluvia, this way. I'm going to introduce you to two stupendous natural poets, who work without a thought to the market, like before, like the real thing. They're going to leave you speechless."

"Speechless," I say.

The ex-minister talks about me as if I'm not right there in front of him. Lluvia is literally dragged to the other side of the patio. As they walk hand in hand, a conga line cuts them off. Abruptly, the music ends and Isaac Delgado himself announces it's time for dinner.

"Ladies and gentlemen, the moment of truth is here. Let's go feast and meet back here in an hour." Applause.

The hordes of guests rush across the garden to reach the tables. The host is about to say something but they abandon him onstage, and though he clinks his Baccarat crystal, few notice he has a few more words.

Oh, eating in Cuba. I think Cubans today enjoy eating more than dancing. I try to join my college friends but it's impossible because they aren't very happy with my presence. In fact, I recognize a few writers from my generation who were friendly in their greetings but, when I try to sit at their tables, the circle closes and there's an awkward, irritated silence.

I've had a very brief career. The truth is I shouldn't be a risk. The real danger is created by politics. "I am the scream and not the echo."

I'm a pest, and my mere presence is contagious, as if my simply standing, breathing, next to them is a problem. When I walk away from the cliques, I hear laughter and whispers behind my back. Why? Why?

Alone, I silently cross that wonderland of trees. I walk until I find the backyard, the circular vegetable patch, the gym, the baths, and I sit down to breathe in the depths of the night by the side of another pool, a smaller one, like a kids' pool, which looks to belong to the original house. At that hour, it resembles a pond where whimsical multicolored fish might play. The sounds of frogs, fireflies, owls, and the polyphonic Vedado soundtrack get mixed up in my head. The champagne and the collective snubs result in a serious dizziness that finds me staring at the bottom of the pond, stunned, where I discover my wavering reflection. I take off my tight heels. I raise my evening dress to my thighs and submerge my feet in the brownish water so I can feel the night enter my body.

I'm alone for a while, trying to figure out why I'd been insisting on staying somewhere I'm not wanted, in a country that's no longer mine, in a city where there's so little left that's recognizable. Does everyone have this argument with their country? Does every citizen reach a moment when they ask if they should continue under its jurisdiction? This isn't very common here; indeed, it's pure treason.

No one should stay for very long where they're rejected,

but I go in circles, aimless in the pool of my own social defeat. I feel like I'm about to drown in my own tears, my own verses, dizzy with my own blah blah blah writings, choking on the suffocating and ever guarded summer haze. Then a hand appears in the dark. I take it without asking questions and rise out of the water. Lluvia is there, watching everything. She dries my tears with a paper napkin and, without asking what's troubling me (in fact, avoiding the subject), she says the tables have assigned seats, and that mine is quite far from hers.

"Well, Cleo, I'll see you in a little while, okay? That way I can tell you about what brings me to Cuba."

"Of course. Don't worry," I say as I pull myself together and straighten my dress, making it seem as if I'm about to join the dinner and thinking that, sooner or later, Cuban authorities will convince her that it would be inconvenient for her to include me in her project . . . But, no, I don't join the dinner. I turn and march straight through a sea of waiters. When I reach the front door, a shadow falls across my path.

"Cleo, are you lost? I'll take you to your table. I've seated you next to some of the folks visiting from exile. Is that all right?" says the host as he takes my hand, making me turn on my own axis, as elegantly as a classical ballerina. He accompanies me so I can't run, sitting me down the way you might punish a little girl, condemning her to a long dinner at the grown-up table.

"Hello everyone. I want to introduce you to a young Cuban writer, by all accounts excellent, though I haven't had the chance to read her myself yet. Her name is Cleo."

Exiles, I think as I take in all those masked and polished people. How would I have turned out if my parents had deserted and I'd grown up in, say, Orlando? It's almost impossible to know. And anyway, during my childhood, what parent could take their child out of the country? We, the children, were hostages.

"Hello," I say, afraid they too won't want me at their table, because for exiles it's also suspect that a woman like me continues to live in Cuba, in spite of everything. I'm trapped between two floors—the elevator of my life has stopped at a dangerous point: the limbo of not being accepted here, and my determination to not leave Cuba. I'm suspect because I'm not intelligible. What should I do? Should I force the door and jump into the abyss so I'll be read, literally, here and there? I don't know.

And these people: Why have they returned? Why now and not before?

The current crisis is a tangible reality. Many come back to reconnect with their old lives, to remodel their old homes, rearrange their affections; they try to rehabilitate their lives among us who, at this point, are just ghosts to them from their pasts.

Others only come to say goodbye to the dying—to all that's dying—overcoming that short and unsustainable distance: Havana–Miami. They slip away on that invisible bridge of water that will take them so far and so near.

But in spite of all the changes, from here, living in *enemy territory* will always be seen as a declaration of war. Once you decide to live there, you'll never again be seen as a trustworthy person; you start to become that target we were taught to shoot at. They'll be suspicious, suspicious, suspicious about you, because you're not some simple American tourist. No, you're a Cuban deserter now among the exile ranks.

Us, the arrow, and them, part of the giant bull's-eye drawn on our heads, aiming always for the *red spot on the scope.*

We've survived the heroic round of the gunshot, we've withstood the crisis, the hurricanes, the political delirium, the harassment, and the distance to give them the welcome they deserve, but in official spaces none of that can be seen as such. To return/visit your homeland/break away. You'd think it would be a pretty straightforward story but, to the military that runs this country, an emigrant is still a traitor.

I sat just as the visitors were removing their masks in order to partake of a cold sautéed lobster soup with onions and curry. In that moment, I realized all their faces were familiar to me. One by one, I recognized the artists, writers, playwrights, and actors surrounding me. I couldn't believe it. I'd seen many of them onstage when I was a child, or on the ICAIC news-reels. Others I only recognized from the back cover photos of books—banned? Covered up? I'd enjoyed the talents of the two women in front of me in Cuban movies from the 1970s.

I didn't dare ask anything. Everything seemed like a dream . . . But no, it was real. I was there listening to their jokes, their sarcasm, and even their awe at their return. My chest felt like it was going to explode. I was at the point of believing that yes, change is possible. The question was in the air and I worked myself up to it. "You've all come back?" I asked in a timid whisper. And the night just flowed; apparently, those had been the magic words, the ones that brought on the smiles, jokes, and anecdotes, confessions, hugs, presentations, coincidences. Two of them had read me and, of course, I'd "read" them too. It was when I was saying goodbye that I realized my real drama: I belonged more to their world than to the one I lived in on the island. And that's a real problem because I hadn't left, but I also wasn't really here.

4

Somebody comes to your door with a "treasure" they've found for you, something so hot, it smokes: a recording of a few of your friends or acquaintances, a little drunk at some party, talking smack about you. In this case, it's the only Havana party I've attended in years, yesterday's party.

I still smell of cigarettes and rum from last night and the consequences are already playing out.

It's noon and I haven't had my first coffee of the day yet, I haven't showered, I haven't brushed my teeth. I'm sitting on the toilet trying to reconstruct faces, dialogues, circumstances. My soul isn't even back in my body yet, and everything's irritating. But it must be time, because there's a knock at the door. I should pull myself together and show my face. They insist, they come at me in the fiercest way to make me confront the raw, revealing truth.

A golden iridescent string appears like an arrow, the smell of cologne breaks through the tiles. The magic string lands and connects me with life: water on water; I wake up and mark my turf. I spring toward the day, filling it with song, the echoes in the bathroom, and the bad news . . . which won't wait.

Oh God/ to raise horses again/ they're nothing/
    more than sad beasts . . .
Radio Reloj, noon in Havana, Cuba; 6 p.m., Madrid,
    Spain;
    6 p.m., Paris, France; 9 a.m., Vancouver, Canada;
    11 a.m., Quito, Ecuador; noon, La Paz, Bolivia; 11:30
    a.m., Caracas, Venezuela; noon, Santiago, Chile;
    5 p.m., London, England;
    11 p.m., Hanoi, Vietnam . . .
    now broadcasting, Radio Reloj, from Havana,
    Cuba . . .
    12:01 p.m., Radio Reloj.

The State Security guy assigned to my family has finally shown up. It's the same charismatic, charming, and almost indispensable guy who sat with us at the dinner table while my mother set traps for him so she wouldn't fall for his ruses. It's the same guy who informed on my parents' experiments and their possibilities of escaping while carrying classified information. There's a very brief moment when Cuban science knows things the intelligence agencies don't know. For reasons of security, they're not told about certain decisive steps. These are delicate moments. And, those, surely, are precisely when Alberto, the "family spy," established the "best" connections between my parents and his superiors.

Which of the recent studies were authorized? Were they on animals or diseased humans? Is the brain an active area of research in Cuba? What are the ethical limits? Has anyone signed a consent form for research in the name of a terminally ill relative? Are unidentified bodies used for research? Are you planning on going to any conferences? Will you see any deserters or relatives during this trip? Do you remember that doctor, also a researcher who defected, the cardiologist who now lives in Puerto Rico? All this was put on the table in the most natural way and, between rum and beer, cigars from the corner store and Populares cigarettes, a chain of jokes would be set loose to get much more out of my mother than a mere laugh.

"Better the devil you know," my mother would say, resigned, her cigarette held high, making rings that would dissolve on contact with her very thin nose and the thick lenses of her seventies-style glasses.

She'd throw out abstract and alarming adjectives just for him, Latin phrases or very rare grammatical constructions straight out of her incomprehensible scientific vocabulary, her very stiff manners marked by how she was raised, and her medical education. My mother never forgot the Hippocratic oath, and maybe that was what saved her from falling into decadence and treason. She had a canon of wisdom and ethics this society could never change, but which it tried to violate time and again. That's how she spent most of her life: on the lookout so she wouldn't lose her way.

My father was the opposite: always silent. He'd sometimes share his rum with the "family spy." When he came by himself to do his questioning, my father, drink in hand, would signal to my mother as if this matter belonged to some other department. His greatest weapon was always delegating.

In my adolescence, all that always seemed like adult stuff, problems between my parents, and a performance that was well beyond me . . . But I was totally wrong. The representation of that betrayal was just the first step in the disintegration of our family. Later, we would have a front-row seat to view the process of our lives falling apart. It's possible everything that happened afterward, even the accident, was a result of Alberto's snitching.

Now I've taken my mother's place. I take a deep breath. I commit myself to her and follow her example. The dinner table isn't set but the guest continues to play out his dangerous role. I don't understand why he visits me. Can I be a real object of persecution? Or is it an old habit, his addiction to informing, that compels him to investigate me? Do they still listen to this man in this country? Is he capable of spying on both artists and scientists? What's his specialty? Are they still using old KGB methods? Why me? Who am I to him, to them?

The techniques have gotten more sophisticated, technology has reached us here, and the "family spy" connects his memory stick to my computer. I make coffee as I listen to the blaring soundtrack from *La fiesta vigilada*.

I try to imitate my mother's gestures, to repeat them as if I were rehearsing a ballet. I try to stay calm and go with the flow . . . Oh! But it's terrible to listen to this bunch of friends and acquaintances, and even strangers, finding the perfect sarcasm to demean what I've achieved.

They ignore how difficult it's been and is to be alive in my right mind.

Jokes, jokes, sarcasm . . . Lies or modifications of the truth.

The recording comes to an end. A profound silence.

It would seem as if my world ends right there and then. I want to flee from my own house, which feels confined and suffocating now.

What am I going to do?

How many times have you itemized your parents' or your friends' shortcomings aloud, or even your own, crying in a lover's bed, or in the quotidian darkness of a friend's room as dawn breaks on a terrible Saturday? This is overwhelming.

What do they want from me? What do they expect from these games of social daggers? To bring me down? To disarm me? Disconnect me from others? To isolate me more and more until I'm speechless? Why is this man at my door with this stick full of voices? What's the endgame after they do us the favor of having us deny the few affections that still survive? How did they record this?

You can recognize the accents. There's irony in the air, and the way they insist on how thin you are, your histrionics, your fears, your weak points, your personal failures, and, above all: your past. Where did Compañero Alberto dig this up? Is it just a coincidence he showed up here with this time bomb in his hands? Should we be grateful to know who's who? Are you a bad person? Did you behave badly enough in your life to deserve this? Shouldn't you try to not damage other people's sacred intimacy? Is this some kind of Decalogue? Or a right violated in the course of the divine and fragile passage of daily living?

I cross the hallway to my studio. I look at a photograph of my mother . . . When the hell have you ever cared what anyone ever said about you? she asks from the picture frame.

Should I thank him? Invite him in for lunch?

No, you can't be grateful to people who do you these kinds of favors. You ask him to leave your house immediately, you kick him out of your life, and push him into the abyss because of what he is, a traitor. But it's too late; you've heard everything.

And your other friends? And the other parties? And the authorities? And you, with you? Where are you?

You look around your living room, check your bedroom, walk around the kitchen, and analyze the layout of your domestic life. They've applied their techniques here too. Where did they put the microphones?

In the picture frames, in the decor, in your clock, in your cell phone, in your stereo equipment . . . Or did you really think they didn't spy on you?

They say this happens in countries all over the world, that it's a question of national security. Matters of state, a priority policy to protect the citizenry.

But, me? Who am I? A small woman who writes things and can't deal with her own fate, much less with State Security or the integrity of the nation.

They record your phone conversations and file them away until they determine you are *not* a danger to the public. Thirty years will go by, your voice will change, you'll lose the last of your loved ones and that's when they'll be done with you. And for what? Who will feel secure because of your insecurity?

Where are the microphones so I can pull them out by the roots? Where are they?

We can't know. Can the *compañero* who records the conversations tell me?

I pick up the phone and ask: "Where are the microphones?"

The truth is that the real microphone—after years of whispering and refraining from saying what you think—the real artifact is already inside you.

5

July came, and with it the clarity of summer. The light in Cuba brings out the real me, all I've tried to keep to myself. Whenever I want to conceal a feeling, a gesture or bittersweet expression that instinctively follows a memory, the natural light makes my inner landscape plain and bares all right in the middle of the street, under unequivocal sunshine. Enlightenment lifts my dress and possesses me. Nothing can be hidden here, not from you nor from others; this island's transparent light tosses secrets about and overcomes them.

The constant olive green and the fiery red, the deep yellow, the moist orange over a range of blues, the scarlet white and violet clouds bleed at dusk, resisting the end of this fatiguing and searing day, defining the emotional patina of a country that constantly cries out how it feels.

It all describes the vulgar symptoms of what it's like to be in Cuba for an entire summer: the taste of mango in your mouth, distilling the crude tropics, iodized, sweet; the gooey Spanish lime and the acidic almond squashed on the sidewalk that now smells of wet earth. Later, at dusk, the crash of a brackish rainbow drives you out of the water because you're afraid of the danger lightning threatens; your mouth is salty; your fingers, wrinkled; you're trembling; and hunger and thirst declare that night is coming. At home, they're waiting for you, or not . . . but it's late. You have to get out of the water.

On your way back, you consider you could have been born in paradise. It's the perennial summer light that causes that vivid and eternal confusion that I carry in my body, and it owns me.

I came home from the beach at about seven in the evening and at nine I could still feel the bland sensation of floating in my ears. I was suffering from the volatility of that delicate film separating the surface from the depths. Those of us who are born here know this is a metaphor, but it would be best to live summer under water.

Few ships and lots of fish. The pain of the rafters who succumbed, the wildest animals, and a damper on all the noise coming from the city. Weightless bodies. Light travels through salt and algae. Your thoughts have been muted so you can resist in real life. There are names careening under your feet and happiness has emigrated forever.

That's what it feels like during my summers on the island.

It's intense to open your eyes and see the shadows above your head. Drunken warriors armed with children and rum. There they go, dancing, their golden bodies kicking about, deformed or perfect, scorched by the sun and by intemperance. You let them go. They free themselves and float up, and you let them go so you can have a moment to yourself.

It's so hard to be alone on a Cuban beach . . . You try to get comfortable on that clear bottom, you pass the murky line, the cold or warm currents, you manage the air in your lungs and put off, in intervals, the hyperrealist surface because, so long as your body can stand to be submerged, you have no reason to go back to the surface.

You propel, you seek out the original phosphorescence, you launch yourself up like an aimless bullet . . . and now, here's the sunny truth: You take a stroke, take deep breaths, and then go down, down, down, once more, abandoning everything. Screams warn you there might be life above but, honestly, you don't care. Real life is happening in your chest, far from Cuba's illusionary stage, that deranged island going around your head, driving you mad, seducing you with all sorts of entanglements and neurosis. It forces you to penetrate the incoherence, invites you to believe it's all logical. It embodies you until it chokes you and drives you to your knees when you emerge. Delirium!

I was trying to make a Cuban-style gazpacho (with whatever's available): melon, onions, stale bread, three small garlic cloves that together are the size of a big one, vinegar, truffle oil I bring in as contraband in my luggage, salt, pepper, seven tomatoes the sun hadn't burned yet and the heat hadn't spoiled, and then, right when I was going to press the button to mix it all in my Russian blender . . . the electricity went out.

A collective wail rose up from the neighborhood. Silence and shadows invaded our street. I remembered I didn't have a single candle to rescue me from the darkness. I should add *candles* to the list of things to bring back from *out there*. There's nothing here. The stores are empty and I barely have enough oxygen to go on.

Too much time surrounded by water and politics, scarcity and socialist stopgaps. A blackout with this heat!

I stretched out on the floor, seeking relief from the cool tiles, slowly undressing my sunstruck body. The day was sticking to me and night had found me golden, burning, alone but intact: lightly served, like a Mediterranean meal, screaming to be tasted, but by whom?

Stretched out and appetizing, distilling, from the ground, the desire the sun leaves on the skin of coastal women, I explored my beautiful old house. In the yard, a slanted section of tiles on the roof allowed me to see the full moon in the sky and then, in the distance, through the windows in the dining room: two art deco buildings, splendid between the trees and the picuala's climbing vines.

"What a waste of sky, of house, of womanliness," I pondered as I curled up on the floor.

They say a little bit of vinegar calms the nerves, relieves the sting, eases the heat on the flesh. After I smeared the balm on my arms, I yanked my white panties off and buried my whole hand in my burning vulva; the wetness facilitated the move and, soaked in honey, I furiously and painfully rubbed my inflamed opening, searching for that rare gem of desire. On my tummy, I tightened my sinewy thighs, opened my legs, and created a bold counterweight against the floor. I came down hard with my pelvis until I felt how this angry rhythm created a kind of circular pleasure, sharp though imperceptible at the start; it was the same pleasure that would later explode penetratingly and exquisitely.

Dazed and delirious, out of my body, I could see my small sex, like a purple mollusk with its distended opening, offering itself to my hands, shivering when touched by my fingers. The thrusting made the pleasure so extreme that it almost killed it, but there were still a few touches left. I love to look at myself and I love touching myself and finding myself fearless. At the end of all this deliciousness, I'd really polished the floor. I left a pool of sweat after my usual final scream. The little animal in me roared, sighed, and surrendered after that romp.

I fell asleep. I don't know if we had two or three hours of darkness, but I woke up when the electricity came back on. It's back! There was light. The blender began to noisily grind. The doorbell screamed insistently. I got up, drowsy, awkward, slipping on my underwear as I made my way to the door.

There he was. The man at the door was none other than Gerónimo Martines, the famous Hollywood actor from Nicaragua. He showed up as if I was waiting for him. Naturally, I welcomed him with a kiss, this Gerónimo who, in this heat, was not exactly the same Gerónimo I'd seen in the movies. He was swimming in sweat, tired, and seemingly lost. What was he doing here? Would he read my poems in . . . ? No, I couldn't believe it.

"Hello," I said as I pulled him inside, where it was illuminated and the light seemed to underscore the impression that I had been waiting for him, or at least waiting for something equally important to shake up my story and take me in another direction, to another turning point, the kind that come now and again in life (every ten minutes), when someone wants something and something or someone becomes an obstacle . . . That's why I recognized him without knowing him, and in spite of the pitch blackness around him on the street, I'll say it again: Even though he didn't look like Gerónimo Martines, I recognized him.

The actor decided to play along with an attitude that said you-act-like-you-know-me-but-shut-up-now-I'm-tired and, though we'd never seen each other before in our lives, we managed that odd whirlwind of emotions. He treated me with familiarity, addressed me casually, and was comfortable by my side. He was wearing a blue sports cap with English lettering, his hair (practically an afro) bulged out at the sides, a comfy-looking loose-fitting black track suit, and a white T-shirt like the kind I wear to sleep. I thought he was overdressed for these temperatures. His sports shoes made him float down the amber hallway and he was so tall that he almost hit the art nouveau hanging lamp in the living room. When the pendulum light bonked him, that's when I thought I'd welcomed Archangel Michael of the Bronx into my house.

"Do you want some gazpacho?" I asked him, following a script from another life.

"Do you have anything stronger?" the actor improvised, now starring in a new chapter of my personal series. His voice was deep. He was rude without being rude. Fringy without being fringy. Yet also smooth as silk, elegant, and a little childish. His accent was very pronounced but he spoke perfect Spanish, a childish Spanish, very musical, perhaps from his mother; I don't know. I showed him my improvised bar in the cupboard and he chose a bottle of Havana Club dark rum that had been forgotten since the last New Year's Eve I'd spent with my parents. As I passed by him and caught a glance of both of us in the enormous mirror that separates the kitchen from the dining room, I realized I was still in my underwear. I excused myself, went to my room to put something on, and returned more or less dressed.

I watched him slowly, calmly, as he drank his rum: He, in turn, watched me savoring the gazpacho right from the blender. I stuck my hand in the jar over and over, running my fingers along the bottom to pick up the lumps that had dripped off the blades. I sucked the broth with gusto.

"Well, say something," I said, smeared with everything. He just smiled, meditating as he grimaced because of the rum's acidity, and looking around at the house from his privileged corner. I realized it wasn't that he was a man of few words, but rather that he was a deep and observant man, perhaps a little shy . . . or, perhaps, if he wasn't saying anything in particular it was because he hadn't come for any special reason. I didn't care if he talked or not. My problem was that I didn't want to be alone between the blackouts, stuck in the family mausoleum, so I went on as usual, as if my visitor was a longtime friend, the guy that comes by every afternoon just to chat. While the actor took his time and drank his dark rum, I washed the utensils, rinsed out my bathing suit, and hung it in the backyard, then swept up the sand I'd tracked in from the passageway around the house. I kept coming and going and he kept checking out the place, but without ever leaving his post. I offered him drinks straight from the bottle and brought out the few ice cubes that had survived the blackout. In the first hour of his visit, we did not speak a word.

Why the hell had he come, and who had given him my address? I don't know, but there he was, calmly drinking my parents' rum, closing that chapter I . . .

"I came to . . ." He tried to speak but the electricity went out again and I think it may have been for the best; it was easier to talk then. "I came so we could talk about your father. I want to make a film about him. I'm looking to start production."

"About my father?"

"Yes, if that's okay by you, of course. I know you don't remember him anymore but, for me, your version of events is important, or whatever you think happened. You're his only daughter, I believe."

"I don't remember *who*?"

"Your father, of course."

"Why wouldn't I remember him?" I asked, disconcerted.

"Well, if you were born in January 1978 and they executed him in July of that same year . . . I don't think . . ."

"Executed him? Oh, for the love of God, no, you're confused. Who are you looking for?" I said, guffawing, then laughing as anxiously as ever.

"You're Cleo, right?"

"Yes, pleased to meet you," I said, holding out my hand from one side of the table to the other, clearing the darkness, touching him one hour after receiving him in my very own home.

"I came so we could talk about him."

"About who? Define 'him,'" I said as I lit a lamp from the literacy campaign, which my mother had kept around since the seventies.

"I'm talking about your father."

"My father wasn't executed. You've been given erroneous information. My father died in a car accident two summers ago," I said, managing to give the dining room a bright and fiery light.

"Are you sure?" he asked, squinting and staring at me with his huge gray eyes.

"Of course . . . do you want to see photos?"

"Are you absolutely sure?" he asked, now with a kind of villain look, delighting in a smile that hid his volatility.

"How could I not be sure?"

"Can I use your computer?"

"Yes, of course," I said, pointing the way to the office next to the kitchen. "But the blackout . . . we'll have to use the laptop. Wait a minute." I got up and came back with the laptop, turned it on, and put in a memory stick in the shape of a whistle, which he'd kept in his track suit's pocket.

The half-light from the computer let me see his rude and perfect face much better. His pronounced cheek bones, the bleak light in his eyes, and even the purplish red of his full lips. There he was, typing away with his meaty fingers, scrolling through his writings, clumsy when it came to the art of finding information to show me who I was and how I fit into his story.

"Since the case of Cuba–U.S. relations isn't closed, it was difficult to get this file from the State Department; it was part of the Cold War archives. There are still unexplained sources and circumstances connected to witness protection programs and other things."

This disclosure confused me even more than the moment when he showed up at the door of my house. Now it turned out I had ties to the State Department? I had no words; I could only feel bombs exploding. Then he started to tell me about the things he hadn't been able to study more thoroughly, but which were also related to the CIA and its Cuban connections. Oh my God, just what I needed. In the morning I'd wake up to the whole block cordoned off and the *compañeros* assigned to me in their white guayabera uniforms, full-time at my door. I'm going to have to cook breakfast, lunch, and dinner just for them until they figure out if I do or don't have anything to do with this. *Everything I make from my writing will go to feeding them,* I thought, a little in jest and a little seriously.

Like a flashback about the future, or a thread of blood that drains and jettisons the story of my life with a dizzying effect, I knew I had been expecting all this for a reason I can't elucidate right now, and I knew it would be a very long night. Seeing my parents' rum had been consumed by Gerónimo in just two hours, I decided to get another bottle from the cupboard, this time a Santiago rum. I opened it, made an offering to whichever saint could help me in that moment, poured a little in a dining room corner, then very responsibly served us each a drink, no ice, neat. I was playing around, but I was serious too, handing him the glass and pulling it back, so he'd tell me what the devil I had to do with these State Department files and, to top it off, the CIA.

I finally gave him his drink. He asked for ice. I indicated the way to the fridge. He got up slowly then took a few steps toward the big white Russian polar bear that, at this hour, was pretty much defrosted. He must have found something there and came back with a few cubes in his glass and a few more to drown in the clearness of my drink. We stared at each other in the dark, and toasted.

His theory—which he explained quickly and gracelessly during the blackout—sounded crazy to me. But what was weird was that he had my birth certificate, knew the exact dates I had started each school, and the exact dates of all my publications.

Why? What other interest could he have in me, in someone so insignificant as me? Why was he leading me on like this? I watched as he put it all together, the genealogy of a life that was supposedly mine and simultaneously foreign, but I couldn't find the logic in his words. His huge hands moved between the darkness and the light emitted by the computer screen.

Later he traversed a family tree and talked about grandmothers, aunts, and a family totally alien to me . . .

I tried to tell myself he really did want something from me but, who was I? Why go through all this trouble to get to me? I'm not a beautiful woman, or sensual, or attractive; I don't have any of the attributes that might be expected to seduce a Hollywood star. While he talked about guerrillas and operations in places like Africa and South America, complicated networks and contacts in the United States, I tried to connect myself to his story, but I'm too scattered and a bit frivolous when it comes to men. I only withdrew to try to imagine his romantic past . . . the thing was, I knew nothing about him; he was a lone wolf. I always get the weird guys. In any case, what could we Cubans know about show business gossip? Nothing, nothing at all. We're out of the loop.

I focused back on the screen, trying to follow his strange story about a Cuban Rambo active during the Cold War, with the cartels, the guerrillas, taking care of business and completing stoic missions, which, to be honest, made no sense to me. All that seemed so foolish, so distant from me. What could I add to these interminable and incendiary adventures by this Mauricio character? I don't like crime stories or action movies. I hate the military and, worse, I hate what the military represents today in this country. The last thing I needed was for

Gerónimo to show up and convince me I'm the offspring of one of them . . .

"That's ridiculous," I said as files started popping open and revealing scanned official documents. In one, there was the name Cleopatra Alejandra (me) but with the surname Rodríguez (from my alleged father) and Mirabal (my mother), a child's fingerprints—mine?—registered in Washington, D.C., the same day as my birthday: January 28, 1978, at three in the morning (the same hour I was born). So many coincidences! The mother: Aurora de la Caridad Mirabal Álvarez . . . and Rodríguez? (my mother), originally from Varadero, Matanzas, born June 30, 1950 (that's correct), a Cuban citizen, married, a doctor by profession. Everything coincided, except the part about me being the daughter of Mauricio Antonio Rodríguez . . . As far as I know, I was born at the Military Hospital in Havana, Cuba, that same January 28 in 1978 that's on the papers. The weird thing is, it says I'm an American citizen.

"To them, my father isn't Rafael Perdiguer, and I'm not Cleopatra Alejandra Perdiguer," I muttered nervously.

"No, according to these official documents, your father is Mauricio Rodríguez, born in Mayarí on January 12, 1942."

Gerónimo talked about all this in a loud voice, translating small bureaucratic matters and the notes at the bottom of the pages from English to Spanish. But there was no information about my father, the one I had known all my life: Why? It also didn't say my mother had ever married anyone but this Mauricio. We reviewed the document together. No, there was no Rafael Perdiguer anywhere.

Could this be a nightmare?

I pulled a chair and sat down next to Gerónimo. I was tired

of standing and I was shaking all over. I saw him trying to find reasons to convince me or to convince himself, and I thought it took a lot of guts to knock on my door, without knowing me, and tell me my father is not my father, that I was born in the very heart of "the enemy," in Washington, D.C., and that, in fact, I was not, at this stage of my life, who I thought I was. Please!

We then looked at my mother's marriage certificate, the one for the marriage to this gentleman whom I'd never once heard talked about in my entire life (and I made sure Gerónimo understood this). It occurred in, of all places, Manzanillo, on October 30, 1969. Not at the clerk's office but at a private home, a family home, but what family? This was so strange. Manzanillo? I never heard her talk about that place. She only talked about Varadero. Always Varadero, to the point that when I think of my mother's birthday, the first thing that comes to mind is the horizon line in Varadero.

Later, he showed me photos of my mother all bundled up in different places in Washington, D.C., and New York, photos of my mother in Havana, before and after my birth, then in Varadero, celebrating a birthday at the home of my grandparents, Bebo and Luisa. More photos at the School of Medicine in Girón, at the Military Hospital, and more recent ones at the brain research laboratory. There were two here at the house, with me and my father, Rafael, the last Mother's Day we celebrated.

"Why would they keep from me that my mother had been to the United States? Are these sources reliable? Who gave you these last photos?" I asked, inconsolable.

"The State Department gave them to me. But tell me . . . don't the dates and the photos match?"

"Yes. But who in Cuba is giving them the information, the recent information, the current news?"

"I would imagine that would be Cuban Intelligence."

"Why would they want to do that?"

"Well, I think there are international agreements, exchanges to assist with clearing up certain issues related to national security. In Rodríguez's case, there must have been long-term agreements, to make sure there would be follow-ups, but I'm only telling you one part. We have a lot, but they have way more and they're not just going to give it to us . . . for now. The files aren't entirely declassified. Some sections are, but some aren't."

"Who executed that man? What did he do?"

Gerónimo looked at me, tired and sleepy.

"It's too long to tell, and I can't believe you don't know who he was. It's better if we meet tomorrow and start from the beginning. To be frank, I thought you knew all this. Would you mind meeting tomorrow? I just arrived today and I'm exhausted," he said, as if he was talking to someone whose entire life wasn't at stake.

At dawn, the other violet hour, the hour of workers and bohemians, strange birds and sleepless seniors, the one for whoever's already awake and those getting ready to sleep, skulking around the beauty of Vedado and the arrogance of its ruins, the actor/director was gone, the foreigner was gone. He abandoned the big house I inherited from my paternal grandparents, those who now, in the short trajectory from night to day, in the deep breath of a broken and hot sunrise, had ceased being kin.

I promised Gerónimo I would check every document until

I found some evidence of any of that absurdity. My otherness, the other me in the fourth dimension. The possibility of being someone else, to have come from someone else, now projected on my body, acting on what had seemed to be the stage of a sweetened real life.

I closed the door and, after saying goodbye to him, was left alone with my everyday routines—except that, at this point, everything of mine seemed borrowed and everyone else's seemed dear. Sleeplessness was stirring my emotions and the rum transported each of my personal dreams to a strange nowhere, an abstract world I'd never explored.

The computer had been left open and the screen showed a photo of my mother kissing Mauricio on the day of her wedding in Manzanillo. It's so awful to not be able to understand a photograph! A photograph is understood through its context, the people in it, the color of its genesis. But I didn't understand. There's not a nerve or emotion that could have moved me when I stood before this image. If the house seemed alien, then my bed was irritating, and that place seemed like a transient hotel, where everything was too big or too small, where I'd been cheated for three decades. "What a nightmare!" I said aloud, exhausted, covering my head, burying myself in my clean sheets, going down, down, down to the core of my dreams until I promised myself I'd get to the bottom of everything, and to the beginning of me.

6

Everything is apocryphal, my life is autofiction, and if I
    write poetry, I return to the original idea . . .
    Certain nights when I'm asleep, the child I was
    returns, that girl you remember who hides under
    my skirt without a handler or a straitjacket.
Everything is apocryphal and I'm a character in an
    unfilmed movie, a version of my wishes that doesn't
    even have my name.

I woke up at two in the afternoon and opened the house to let in
the light. I wanted the sun to wipe away everything Gerónimo
had told me. I turned on the shower and, under the stream, I
swore to not see him again and, even better, to not revisit the
subject at all. Not to think, not to feel, and, more precisely, not
to be. Why did I want to be what I'd never been or to know
something my mother didn't want me to know? At this stage,
I'd look pretty silly searching for a father. I opened the French
doors and stepped from the bathroom to the bedroom, where I
saw myself in each of the giant mirrors. Seven versions reflected
me back as an intruder. I shook my head, splattering water all

over the room, rubbed my skull with the towel, and returned to myself.

I prepared my escape. I'd go away to the provinces for three weeks. For years, I'd been promising myself a trip through Cuba so I could check out how things were going, because Havana is legendary compared to how people live in the countryside. I wanted to go to Oriente; I'd never been to Baracoa. I dug up my little military suitcase and began to pack some camping clothes, a small first aid kit, bug repellent, cans of food . . . I wanted to leave as soon as possible. Gerónimo would not be able to find me upon his return. Hadn't I wanted to start writing prose? Well, first I needed to figure out how . . .

There was a sudden explosion on my block. The dark hall-way was lit in a flash and I suddenly had six people—or, rather, six off-duty police officers—breaking into my house.

THE SEARCH

I try not to feel watched
To not listen to that neurotic melody
But they're following me   I know because of the me
    that's missing
in the objects disturbed
They take your heart from your home
Toss your documents and attachments
Kill the spirit of the photographs
Break your circle of trust
Inspect your coats and behead your toys
You undress between translucent walls
Live marked filmed overheard

They peel your image from mirrors   exile your soul
in-xile your being
Rattle the innate order of things
Discover your weaknesses and work the wound until it
    becomes a scar
You always thought you were nothing
but now you are
that nothing's nothing.

There's a brusque knock at the door. If you don't open it, they change their tactics: a good kick or a set of elegant master keys will serve to unlock it, depending on whether you're a Cuban citizen without rights or a chance of being heard at any level, or, instead, if you're a diplomat or some other kind of foreigner who can file a legal complaint. The methods vary, depending on whether anyone will mourn your death or if you're a common and helpless mortal, in which case they destroy everything. If you're someone who matters to them, then they'll do it with care.

Do they want you to know, or not, whether they're carrying out a search on you? They might come while you're gone. They might take your hard drive and bring it back so stealthily you'll never know it was gone. Or they can tear your house apart, to make it obvious, scare you, stop you dead in your tracks. Those days of terror will help you reconsider if you should or shouldn't be doing whatever you're doing, be involved in whatever you're involved in. What am I involved in?

The problem comes when I'm not involved in anything and they come and threaten me over what I might be thinking or writing.

The entire operation depends on the initial purpose of the raid. Although, in fact, there are the usual, classic domestic raids. For example, everything I'm writing right now will be checked by my housekeeper tomorrow or Monday. She knows I know but we share this "dark splendor" knowing that, just by writing, I'm risking my life and that, without her, my life would be much more complicated . . . It doesn't have to reach the level of a raid. It's always better if the housekeeper takes care of informing on your movements and calming them down; otherwise, it can get too violent. The next level is the "family spy," like the one I'm always talking about, the lifelong friend, the guy who reads over your poems, helps you prepare the materials for national and international contests. He types your manuscripts and takes your memory stick so he can print things up for you, because your printer has unexpectedly stopped working. That's who, even if he loves you, keeps the members of State Security up to date on your case. He knows you know. You feed him, you love him, you help him with everything because it's always better that the case is in his hands and not in those of a complete stranger.

They also have a way of reading your email, but I don't have an Internet connection at my house. I live surrounded by books and ghosts. I'm alone and I only rarely get calls from editors of different translations who ask me if I want to go out and get some air so I won't suffocate in here.

My poetry is my magic protector against fear; if I write, if I read poetry, if I recite poetry to myself, in silence or in a whisper, like a mantra, I know nothing will happen to me. At a table in Córdoba, seated next to Herta Müller, I once heard her say she recited poetry to herself whenever she was taken to the Securitate for interrogations. I turn to Eliseo Diego for prayers when the interrogations start at the airport, during raids, and during the daily sequence of fears. One of Eliseo's poems, then one of mine, one of Eliseo's poems, then one of mine. That's how I calm down, that's how I keep myself from being disarmed as they try to neutralize me.

Among the ranks of State Security, there are those with degrees in literature, history, linguistics, physics; there are writers, singers, philologists, scientists, psychiatrists, mechanics, philosophers. "We have the most cultured prostitutes in the world," according to Fidel in one of his most extensive speeches, along with the most well-prepared doctors, the most literate people in the world. What we don't have here is the chance to build our own world; therefore, everything we do—the good and the bad—is entirely deliberate, and that's what terrifies me. On this militarized island full of farewells, we're trapped between conformity and defecting. We Cubans have been well trained; our real damage is in our souls. Innocence isn't possible here.

Hardly anyone visits this house since my parents died, just the housekeeper (the same one for the last thirty years), who has come back to work three days a week, so she must have skipped something or done something wrong for them to break in like this, in such a violent way, and scared a woman alone, defenseless, who is neither brave nor possessed of the stuff of heroes. What could I do against them?

I stood in the middle of the hallway, as if I were waiting for the worst, numb. I let them come and go all over the house. Anyway, this house isn't my house anymore. I know that.

First, they searched behind several paintings, using these strange little gadgets I'd never seen before.

Then they asked questions:

1. About my computer. (I handed it directly to the officer in charge of the raid.)

2. About the suitcase filled with clothes, food, and medicines: "And where is our little *compañera* headed?" ("To Oriente.") "Why." ("Just because.")

3. About Gerónimo, his intentions, and how many times he'd been in contact with me, here or abroad. (What could I say? Nothing. Even I don't quite understand what's going on.)

4. About the photos, or the family album. (I handed them all over, every single one.)

5. About the liquids and substances I imbibe that can be found on the premises. (There was very little liquor and they took it . . . to analyze it?)

I only asked one question, to which they responded with laughter.

"Do you have a court order?" It was probably too late: The house was already upside down.

One of the officers, the one assigned to read the files in my computer, read my poems in a mocking voice, dying of laughter, defiant and ironic. He gave the reading the same intonation as the morning announcements at an elementary school. They checked my videos, my photos, they filmed my room, took an inventory of what was in the fridge, the cash, and everything I had in the pantry. They took the phone receipts and asked me about the very few calls I had jotted down. They checked the electric bill, the gas bill, even the water bill.

They read a list of names to me and asked me to nod my head if I recognized any of them. No, I didn't know anybody. Then they showed me images of those same people taken in my own home . . .

Their harassment became increasingly intense. They threw all my clothes to the floor (it was curious to see my under-wear tangled with the books that had my name on them). They searched the books in a very detailed way and a photo was taken of each cover by the raiding party technician.

They charged the little gadgets again. By then I understood they were cameras and microphones.

After they left, I felt exposed, naked, empty. There were still questions which, though unanswerable, I preferred to keep quiet: Why do this to me? Who am I to them? Above all, who am I to me? Why doesn't anyone visit me since my parents died? Who can tell me? Who that doesn't experience this fear?

Márgara, our housekeeper since time began, has been a shadow that silently flutters through the house like a black butterfly. I have no memory of my mother cleaning or cooking. It was always Márgara who helped us, never once missing a day.

She's a mature woman, tall, slender, black, and sinewy, who moves the heaviest furniture without breaking a sweat, and skates barefoot around the house with the broom, shining the wet floors without losing her balance. She doesn't speak, or says very little, a silence she imposes. There's never a need to complain or to ask her to do what only she knows how to do.

Márgara brought a bowl of chicken soup to the table, put it

in front of me, then sliced a lemon and squeezed it right into the broth.

What am I doing here? I thought, *I'm exposed on a reality show, on a stage I once believed was my house now filled with cameras and microphones.*

"We're being filmed, Márgara," I explained to her. "Everything we do is being watched someplace else."

She simply nodded and continued with her daily routines. She made my bed and left at dusk, the house clean, everything in its place.

How can I go on living with this lack of privacy, crossing this long stretch of autofiction, sharing my life with everyone and no one?

When I put my head down on my pillow and felt the intense scent of the laundry soap—the one boiled in the yard, made with charcoal and potassium to swallow the dirt, the same yellow soap used by Barbarito Díez—I returned to my original sentiment: This is my house and these are my white sheets. As I tried to accommodate my bones on the mattress, I found some papers under the pillows. They were my poems—but what were they doing there? Márgara had just changed the linens. I sat up to read them and discovered two copies of each poem, my text and a different version of each.

Where I had said *exile*, it now said *delirium*.

Where I had said *fear*, it now said *ice*.

Where I had written *fascist abyss*, it now said *guttural abyss*.

Where I had put *enclosure*, someone had written *winter*. There were copies of more than twenty of my texts and at the end, a blank sheet with Márgara's handwriting, which until then I'd seen only on grocery lists and telephone messages. It was a warning.

"I've changed them for your own good. Forgive me, but I had no other choice. Take care of yourself and let's never speak of this. Márgara."

7

I was on all fours and I'd lost track of my heartbeat and any notion of time when I let Gerónimo mount me by throwing all six feet of his body on mine. His weight was part of the ecstasy, and the effort of holding him up on my back kept me distended, potent, as tense as a harp string. I fit around his sex like a glove from behind. He threaded it softly until it reached a magnificent curve and clenched. He raved between assaults, just touching the head of the diamond, provoking a sharp torrent of joy, all the while tapping little explosions, rockets of pleasure, swells that came and went, riding the onslaught of lights and exultation, shattering fiercely and wet at the end of combat. With my mind blank, crazed with his smell, smeared with his sweat and holy water, I'd wake up between orgasms just to look at the artifacts on the wall. I felt like a traitor for not telling him they were taping us, spying on us, watching us. I'd retreat to pleasure, trying not to think about the eye on us. I'd return to the den that was my body, rise with the sway of his efforts and convulsions, then go back to the interminable mortification I complied with on all fours, with my knees on fire, buried and bruised by the bedsprings, feeling him tremble as he surrendered to the power of my bones.

If you've played a keyboard boosted by lead counterweights at the ends of the keys, you've felt the tension designed to train and strengthen the fingers, and you know just how hard it is to pluck music out of that. You know pleasure hurts, but it also transports when the music flows in spite of the pain.

"Gerónimo, they're watching us," I said between whimpers, extending my knees, letting my body drop on the mattress, making him fall on top of me as if he'd just leapt from the second to the first floor.

"Where? Who?" asked Gerónimo, sitting up, scared.

"The cameras. They're there."

"Okay, okay . . . take it easy. Don't scare me like that. I thought there was someone in the room."

"Well, who knows how many of them are watching this from wherever. Don't you care?"

"Cleo, I'm so used to cameras, to the paparazzi, to friends who sell your life to the tabloids . . . Anyway, they're probably disconnected. It was probably just a threat . . . Turn over, please. I love looking at your back," he said, peeling off his T-shirt and throwing it on the nearest piece of furniture before turning back to my ass with his fine lust.

Making love in front of the cameras, showing off your nakedness in the privacy of your room, undressing for the multitudes in your childhood hideaway, the place where you spent your fevers, your adolescence, your nightmares, your games, and your most secret tribulations—where I hide my weeping, my obsessions, my joys, and my defeats—making love with Gerónimo in all possible positions in front of the camera, with my back to the camera and as I'm peaking, nearing heaven, always aware we're being watched. The walls of my room are viewed from who knows where in this city, a place where other men and women share the crumbs of our intimacy.

Gerónimo is asleep between my legs. I'm in that lethargic state between sleep and bliss. Today, the room is like a baseball stadium. We've been blindfolded, the bed is in the middle of a field. Completely exposed in the box, we possess each other. And from there, the public watches the game without scruples. We are blindfolded and they see it as a drill, emotionless, which is why, in the pocket created by our bodies, everything is happening as if we were alone.

At dawn, I get up and head straight to the shower. Although Cuban women usually shower at night, my mother taught me to shower twice a day. Gerónimo and I have very different habits. He shuts himself in my parents' bathroom for hours while I poop and pee, and, in fact, take a shower with the door open. I walk through the house dripping water, thinking about what I'm going to write, and in every corner where I see a camera, I stick my tongue out and mutter a good morning to whoever is spying on us.

When I open my computer to read over my Word docs, I realize nothing of what I've written this week is there; everything's disappeared. Shaking, I check each and every file. I need to know how far back the disappearances go. There's nothing in my computer. I slam it shut. I watch Gerónimo making coffee in the kitchen, his hair wet, his body relaxed. He's singing in English and his serenity doesn't deserve to be interrupted by my misfortune. I think maybe this is a mistake, a nightmare, and I go back to my laptop, open it, stick my face in the screen.

I'm looking for just one verse, one note, but there's nothing, nothing.

I try to cry but I can't. I try to run but my legs won't respond. Everything has been erased from my computer. I try to recall my poems but I don't usually memorize my texts. To recall them strikes me as atrocious and ridiculous as losing them.

"I don't remember my poems," I tell Gerónimo, annoyed as I take the warm mug he offers me.

"Very few writers remember their work."

"They've disappeared. There's nothing here," I say as I open my laptop, showing him the empty blue of the screen. I'm terrified and drink my coffee quickly, still hoping to find something.

Incredulous, Gerónimo looks at the computer while I dedicate some time to staring at the dregs at the bottom of my cup. There are people who say they can read the future in what's left there; they say that in the morphology of that mud, of that chipped surface, your destiny is written. The weird thing about mine is that there isn't much except some scattered powder, and at the very bottom, a few illegible coffee shavings and nothing more.

"Cleo, there's nothing. The computer's as empty as if it were brand new. Are you sure this is where we downloaded my files?"

I just look at him, seriously, shooting off a pair of flames from my eyes to his.

"It can't be," he says, searching all over the machine, looking at me resentfully, but admitting, for the first time, that it might be worthwhile to believe my exaggerations.

★

Márgara arrived early, saying good morning from the door so as to announce her presence. She found me in bed, in a deep depression, unlike any since the death of my parents. She picked up around the bed as if I wasn't in it. She got me up just to change the sheets, then laid me back down, arranging me on the pillow, and tucked me in.

She got the pressure cooker going and soon the house was filled with an intense haze of red beans. The sound of the pressure cooker is the sound of Cubanness. It's the soundtrack against hunger in every home in this country. It's an asthmatic tone, intermittent and eternal, and it sounds like real life.

She made café con leche with a little bit of sugar and a dash of salt, the way my father used to make it. She fried up some green plantains with garlic, then smashed them—called "magolla"— that's what's for breakfast in certain parts of Oriente. She's from there and, from what I can see, so is my alleged father.

Then she looked for all the printed poems dispersed throughout the house, including the ones she'd blotted out to fool the censors, and, once the table was set with a linen tablecloth and silver utensils, Czech beer mugs to drink Cristal, and little dessert spoons for no dessert, she set them down.

When Gerónimo arrived, sweaty and starved, we sat down to eat. Everything seemed normal, as if he and I had lived together in that house for decades, but no, he'd just recently moved in because there's no privacy in Cuban hotels. And is there any in this house? Privacy on this island is like winter or snow, an illusion.

Gerónimo, so Americanized, didn't quite understand the ritual of dining with Márgara, who'd already displaced me from the head of the table to accommodate the actor. This machismo-

Leninism is incomprehensible to a man who's used to living with the deep feminism of his colleagues. But none of that seemed important in the moment because his efforts to try and access the national history archives via an official request had been denied by the authorities. The response had been a resounding "no" without any diplomacy or courtesy.

"You might have two Oscars and the support of the public, the press, and international media at your feet, but here, Compañero Gerónimo, we are not interested. And, no, my friend, you're not getting into the history archive and that's that," I said, imitating a growling military officer, curt and disagreeable.

"How can I make a film about that man without doing research in those archives? It wouldn't be a serious project."

In Cuba, when things go wrong, people usually get drunk, go to sleep, or make love. Gerónimo went to bed immediately to wait for me but I stayed behind looking over the copies Márgara had recovered for me.

"Thank you, Márgara," I said, on the verge of tears. "But this is nothing. I've lost two years' worth of work."

I opened my computer, as if to copy them, but my own laptop no longer seemed trustworthy. I stared at the blank bluish white file as if my poems could just appear there. Like a child, I was determined to change the ending of the story. Two big tears dropped from my eyes just as Márgara came and stood in front of me.

"Copy this, miss, copy this."

A CAGE WITHIN

And she who is I wants to open the cage
cage that separates me from the living

But we were already   yes   a bit dead what
    with everything and birds hungry for light
Dead from all the words silenced in the
    darkness   you have reached us
Ready to predict from the learned confinement
I strive to translate with vigor my letters engraved on
    the body.

TOY CAGE

I see traps along the way
but they look like flowers   compasses or mirrors
The collection of cages I inherited from my mother
    made me female
I fell as low as the deep sound of my orchestra
That's where I'm going   arrogant and enslaved
The onslaught promises the worst
Girl   toy cage
My virgin heart   flushed   doesn't
    inherit insult or pain
And it's just that there are no cages inside the body
    of a girl.

At six-thirty in the evening, when Gerónimo awoke from his nap, Márgara was still standing at attention in front of me, dictating my lost poems from memory. She'd recite my version and then the one she'd deemed respectable for the authorities; out of respect, I copied both. I'd rarely heard her voice so clearly but this time her tone was firm, like a *pionera* with her morning pledge in elementary school. She declaimed them with meaning, her meaning on my words, even though she knew all those phrases were implicating her.

The image of that tall, muscular black woman, ramrod straight while reciting texts at dusk, impressed Gerónimo, who decided to open one of his whiskey bottles, the ones he had brought from L.A. so he could toast to everything he found surreal and fascinating.

Márgara finally left at eight in the evening. She closed the door with a whisper I thought I could make out.

"Take care of yourself, because I won't live forever."

Gerónimo and I lay down on the fresh tiles and, without a word, we made love with our clothes on under the eyes of the cameras. We didn't turn on the light, which was slowly ebbing, like the day from our bodies.

"FUMIGATION! Public Health. FUMIGATION!"

That was the first thing I heard when I opened my eyes. The sound of an engine, a penetrating smell of kerosene, and a sense that the smoke would swallow us at any moment if we didn't flee the house immediately. Gerónimo threw his bathrobe on and I pulled on a pair of shorts and one of his shirts. We ran to open the door but the cannons were already shooting out all over the lateral hallways and the smoke wouldn't let us breathe. We were under siege.

The armed group entered the house. Somebody needed to guide them through the labyrinth but breathing in that smoke was worse than watching to make sure they didn't steal from us or shoot poison at our belongings. It didn't matter anyway. We've been vulnerable so many times before . . . We sat down on the sidewalk, right across the street from the house, to watch, from the first terrace on, the penetration into our intimate space.

We stayed there for half an hour, waiting for the insecticide to dry and for the air to clear inside the house. Amid the fog, we saw Márgara go in. The dark of her body pushed into the snowy smoke until she disappeared, like nothing, into the scattering clouds. Márgara is so well trained; she's bulletproof.

"There's a new battle here every day, right? How funny! They keep you on your toes, alert, entertained, figuring out a new complication every hour . . . What if we looked for one of those cameras? What do you think?"

"But we already know where the cameras are," I said, mortified.

Márgara appeared on the terrace with two mugs of café con leche. I crossed the street to get the tray, gave her a grateful kiss, and asked her to please get out of the house and breathe for a while. She refused because there was too much work to do in the house and she was already behind. When I got back to the sidewalk, I discovered Alberto talking to Gerónimo as if they were old friends. The "family spy" was reclaiming our lives again. I wanted to warn Gerónimo but it seemed I was too late.

We forgive our kidnapper time and again, we rationalize him, take him back again into our lives. We even celebrate his birthday, as if that date wasn't, in a way, the anniversary of our own burial. So there we were, opening a bottle of Chivas with Alberto. Why? Because he turned fifty today; because he deceived Gerónimo by telling him that when it came to the archives, where he'd spent two years of his social service duty, and where they'd told Gerónimo he couldn't access the information no matter how important a Hollywood actor he might be, he was the person who'd solve the dilemma, "underground" style. This is the same Alberto who, today, coincidentally happens to turn fifty, and in case I don't believe him, he shows me his ID, and just in case I want to add one more sentimental element to the narrative . . .

"What's today, Cleopatra Alejandra?"

"August ninth."

"So what happened on a day like today?"

"You were born," I said with disgust.

"And what else, pretty girl? Guess!" he said, pinching my cheeks.

"I don't know," I said, brusquely pushing him away.

"On a day like today, your parents got married. We have to celebrate. Don't you think, Gerónimo?" he said, proudly showing him a photograph of my parents' wedding; that is, my mother and the man they claim is my father.

Gerónimo couldn't tell this was all a prepared performance, that the photo was the sign of entrapment, since no one ever remembers someone else's anniversary, much less walks around with their wedding picture.

"I brought it, precisely, to celebrate . . ."

Gerónimo was delighted and he continued to toast and listen to Alberto's bluffing about my parents. He was taking notes, asking him questions I could have answered without the histrionics. It's one of the characteristics of those who attend to us to make themselves useful, to arrive in the nick of time, to be with us during our difficult periods and encourage us when all seems lost. Alberto is very charismatic, and I only really realized it when I saw a great actor fall completely under his spell.

Isn't Cuba an excessively hallucinatory place, with its hidden and visible demons; its mangos dripping in the sun; the smell of picadillo a la habanera made with something that looks like meat and that Márgara prepares in our kitchen; the avocados perspiring on a shelf; boiled corn; blackened plantains, almost rotted and hanging in the patio; the ravings about the sea that rum provokes and our heads imagine, imagine leaving by sea?

Isn't this unreality and what it exudes crazy enough for Gerónimo, surrounded by cameras and awkward and unprecedented circumstances, to accept a joint from our beloved and unpredictable, infinite Alberto?

"In socialism, no one knows the past that awaits them," and I know perfectly well this smoke will turn to tragedy.

8

I've been sitting on this marble bench for more than three hours. This feels like a mausoleum. How can our highest leaders contemplate the political panorama from here? This height is uncomfortable. You have to be careful not to fall from the vertigo, and to hold yourself up is painful.

Gerónimo was authorized to meet with the history archive's new director. He's waited months for this meeting; he's come to visit month after month but they've refused to see him. Finally, they let him in the doors today.

How long will this take? Will they let him look through the archive? Do documents about that man exist? Did that man exist?

From the time I was little, I've walked, danced, paraded through, in cars and with my gaze, the Plaza of the Revolution. But it looks different today, because winter in Havana softens the character of the drama we interpret. Everything is clear. Today, I find a kind of cynical lyricism in these symbols. The guards watch me from a distance as a copy of yesterday's newspaper and a yellow butterfly float by. This silence is so heavy that I can see the traces of the parades on the ground. I see our entire lives being swept away, dragged along, tossed into a rolling trash can.

Our existence has been one grand parade that, in the end, transforms into a frenetic conga line. Just as it seems we're going to shatter, to rebel against the effrontery, against the lies projected on the buildings around this plaza, we end up dancing, drunk on politics and dazzled by fear.

First there's the parade, then the party—bread and circus—beer and live music, and then later, bending bodies under the stream of water, letting those cold needles prick, pierce, and pin your back to the wall.

Moonshine, doubt, and rum's devilish spirit come to interrogate you. Memories, perpetual flight, and the fear of escaping, or not, of not knowing what's right—these bring you to a standstill. The water purifies your tears and a whimper swallows your guilt at being both spectator and participant in this circus. The speech and the conga line go down the drain. You fall, fall, fall knowing one day you won't be able to get up and away from the danger. You know your parents couldn't either because it was too late to cure the sickness we all suffer.

We live one on top of the other, and this overcrowding, this need for our neighbors in order to survive is both contagious and debilitating; we end up fighting; we divide until we fall into a deep loneliness, surrounded by witnesses.

I'm sitting on the bench, looking out at the panorama before me, an empty Plaza of the Revolution. José Martí's gaze is aimed somewhere else, maybe out to sea—it rises above the disaster, beyond this. I feel very small here, beneath the grayness and its shadows, waiting for them to let Gerónimo have a handful of crumbs of our historic memory.

Gerónimo finally crosses the esplanade in the company of a

military officer. First post, second post, third post, a leap to the sidewalk, and then he finally hugs me.

It's so hard to experience anything on a human scale in this plaza . . . under siege?

Before, it was the Civic Plaza, today the Plaza of the Revolution . . . and tomorrow?

We're tomorrow. Nobody is in charge of today, no one prepares for the transition. Tomorrow is today and the future doesn't exist because those who govern us know they're living their own futures now.

Gerónimo kisses me and, slowly, as if he's caressing my ear with his voice, tells me we have to fly to Mexico. There's nothing here. The information has disappeared. Off the record, they say everything's with Gabriel García Márquez, because he wanted to write a book about this same man and the information was given to him. It's not certain but we have to ascertain if that's true.

"But who can get to García Márquez?"

"I can," says Gerónimo, resolute, looking me right in the eye, reminding me that he received several awards and nominations for his interpretation of Aureliano Buendía in the movies.

"Will I get to meet García Márquez?"

"Of course. Do you think he'll have the information, or do you think they're trying to distract me with something they consider impossible?"

"I think García Márquez works in a different kind of writing. I don't think any of this is true but . . ."

"But you'll meet García Márquez . . . and we'll get to the bottom of this."

A car with mounted loudspeakers runs a sound check as it circles around the well-guarded ministries. A hymn plays over the plaza as several Japanese tourists film Che, strewn on a gloomy polished granite wall where, ever since I learned to read, it says, "Until Victory Always." Then one of the Japanese tourists' telephoto lenses discovers Gerónimo. The tourist group approaches us like a threat, armed with cameras of all sizes. They come toward us as the rain intensifies, blurring their vision, which allows us to escape to the Teatro Nacional's terrace. This January storm has overwhelmed the bodies on the plaza. We kiss under the almond trees. The cold is dangerous in Cuba. The water soaks through to your bones, the humidity sneaks into your body until you're sick. The tropical salt will also make you ill. Havana looks like a movie set now, and I realize that's what it's been ever since I can remember: a big black-and-white set, the stage on which we Cubans pose as extras. Now, and only now, do we feel a little like lead players.

I'll meet García Márquez, I thought as I shivered from the cold. We crossed under Martí's shadow on the esplanade, breaking with the ghosts of the patriots who've always paralyzed me. I yank down these specters, I rip them up as if they were cellophane; in my mind, I tear them up. I push and crush them. They fall in my way as I run, run, run under the downpour trying to flag down a taxi, latched on to Gerónimo's hand, who, little by little, learns how to hold me and guide me between the rain and these fictions.

★

To ask for a visa for a Cuban is to beg.

To ask for visa for a Cuban is to plead, to feel helpless before the face of a Mexican woman who doesn't want to believe you do anything else with your life except sleep with a foreigner so you can run away from the socialist inferno.

What is a consul?

In Cuba, a consul is not a public employee, a consul is a king treated with reverence because the consul has the key to that other dimension.

To ask for a visa in Cuba fills me with such shame.

They ask me things that have nothing to do with the matter at hand. Do they ask the same questions of all the citizens who make it this far?

It's been a long time since I've been out of Cuba. I need to breathe a little. I need to meet that Nobel winner. But I hate going through this. Is it worth it to talk about yourself, to turn yourself in just to get the entry permit for anywhere else in the world? I'd give it all up if I didn't have to respond to one more question.

The Mexican consul has doubts about me, and I, honestly, doubt these questions are necessary. Your privacy, your integrity is on the table.

What would happen if I requested asylum in Mexico? Thousands of citizens flee Mexico daily.

What would happen if I used Mexico as a bridge to the United States? Thousands of Cubans cross that border daily. I'd be one more tear in a sea of emigrants.

The letter of invitation says I'm going to one of my book releases, but that's not true. My last book was already released and promoted in Mexico. Why am I lying? Why do we lie? Is lying the only honest way to get out of Cuba? We lie to Cuban authorities, we lie to international authorities. From the time we're kids, we Cubans are taught how to sharpen our double-speak to survive.

Gerónimo is on the other side of the office talking to the ambassador. Only glass separates us. I can hear everything. They're talking about a story that was never filmed concerning Trotsky's assassin. Would Leonardo Padura sell the rights? Who would direct the movie? I've always wondered. Gerónimo and the ambassador talk freely. When you're born in captivity, you have a very precise set of gestures. But when you're born free, you have a certain looseness, a way of being without reservation or anxiety.

The interview is long. Now and again, the ambassador glances my way. The consul takes delight in my vulnerability during the interview and savors torturing me.

"How many times have you been to Mexico? How many books have you sold there? What cities have you been to? Do you have family in the United States? Where did you meet Gerónimo?" asks the consul, knowing my letter and I are lying.

"At my front door," I say, telling the truth for the first time.

"What did he come to Cuba for?"

This is the kind of situation that stirs my paranoia and I cease to care about anything. I get up from the chair, ready to walk out the door without having gotten my exit to the sea. This is precisely the point when you can't take any more, the impasse when you can't tell anymore if the diplomatic corps is at the service of State Security or if this woman just wants to pick up some typical tabloid gossip.

"Visa granted!" she says in a loud voice as she greets the ambassador with a wink. Gerónimo comes in and shakes her hand. She leans her face forward and steals a kiss, and then a photo, and with the photo, his soul.

We leave the embassy in silence. One more complaint and Gerónimo is going to run.

I'm imprisoned, completely imprisoned; my freedom always depends on so many circumstances, people, positions, institutions, goodwill, and political will that, even with visa in hand, it's hard for me to believe that in one week I will finally be able to leave again. This time, with Gerónimo.

9

On my desk—which was for decades my parents' desk, this dark and horrible looking monstrosity, an essential part of the so-called "Spanish remorse," that dose of bad taste generations of Cubans inherited and have in our homes without ever knowing who could have ever loved something so somber—on this enormous piece of furniture with polished lions on the drawer handles and plumes and helmets and conquerors with invasive looks on their faces assaulting our kingdom; here, on this desk, where what was inside human skulls and their experimental fates was jotted down in the clinical histories of the dead patients my parents analyzed; right here on this horizontal plane where I stop to work every morning, that's where I drop the two poetry collections I picked up from the Book Institute.

They weren't accepted for publication. Why? Censorship and the censor have a singular partnership in Cuba. No one ever knows who evaluates you, and no one will ever know why that unknown person has censored you. A secretary receives and returns your original or originals as she talks to her daughter on the phone about what to make for dinner tonight.

Are they punishing you or your books? Is it your ideas or your attitude they're censoring? Is there actually somebody in that office of prohibitions, or is it just a secretary who receives and returns books that are never read?

Is it you who's persecuted or is it really that they're after you for your ideas?

And what ideas? I have a lot of ideas about each of these matters. Is poetry really a threat to this country? Aren't you really persecuting yourself?

What kills censored writers, whether expatriated or ostracized, is autophagy. Many end up stuck between political envy and literary envy. You have to learn to fly over the country's literary and political map to heal your mind and write without fear, but the only way to do that is by working.

How do you know if you've been officially censored?

The writers who don't see our work published in our homelands in a timely way, who are kept apart from the cultural process of our countries of origin—we end up talking to and about ourselves, making protagonists out of our tormentors. We end up sealed like a strongbox, fighting with invisible enemies, writing about this very thing in all our novels, stuck in the elevator of fear, breaking off communication with everything that connected us to that other reality, the one where the rest of the mortals live. Monothematic and neurotic, we Cuban writers go crazy or grow ill with irreversible conditions. We lose our center, we get lost, we give up, we're beaten by mediocrity, by terror, and, above all else, by the sickness that is Cuba.

In my parents' conceptual lab, I open the censor's cranium and, like in *Fantastic Voyage*, I enter the officer's displaced brain. In his Turkish saddle palpitate the suspicions that only he knows about. Bit by bit, my images encircle his head as if it were a plaza under siege. Perhaps my genetic material will contaminate the diagnosis; the chemical weapons to silence me are in the medical prescription.

A decade or two from now, under another censorship land-scape, when my words have aged enough for this military administration that's been forced to work in culture, then I'll be able to publish my verses. For now, silence and fear.

As if in a museum, two poetry collections rest on my parents' desk, translated into various languages . . . except Cuban Spanish.

Censorship doesn't exist, my love; censorship doesn't exist, my; censorship doesn't exist; censorship doesn't; censorship . . . shhhhhh.

With the equipment Gerónimo brought for the interviews he hasn't been able to set up because he can't find the right witnesses for his story, and with some things I had at home that were my parents or mine, Russian or German Democratic, and including two gadgets Alberto gave me, we've built an installation in the living room of my house.

The poets' voices hang from the ceiling, banned Cuban writers reading their own novels or censored poems. In the very middle, my voice reads the two poetry collections prohibited or simply ignored by the Book Institute. Fifteen headphones sway overhead. The voices are activated when you touch the headphone and stop to listen.

Not all censored writers are represented but you can hear Reinaldo Arenas, Guillermo Cabrera Infante, Heberto Padilla, and José Lezama Lima in their crudest silence. You can also hear voices that sound familiar but never were, because of censorship. Gerónimo has also read some of these writers' works in English. His voice is deep, pained. It's stunning to hear them in a different language.

People knock on the door at all hours to listen to the voices. At dawn, we become aware of the bell: some young people want to hear the banned texts. Because our private exhibition is called "Censorship," we open the door no matter the hour so nothing is "censored." The wires move like pendulums wanting to scream their truth. Under the headphones, someone gets the idea.

How long will this installation make sense in this living room, this city, this island, in me?

In the living room, a murmur of voices invades the silence. The murmur recalls a mantra to keep the censorship at bay; it can be heard on the streets. A group of young people waiting in a short line are dispersed by the neighborhood cop; that's why it's better to come at night, when the silence lets you listen, without repression, to the details and the voices of the lost poets.

10

It's worth it to go through the distasteful experience of being searched and questioned by the officers who serve at José Martí airport in Havana. It'll always be worth it to feel those eyes going over your life and those hands burying themselves in your luggage or your body. It's worth it to explain yourself to a camera or military officer who doesn't understand, who can't tell the difference between the rule and the exception. It's all worth it, absolutely all of it, just to get out and breathe for a while.

When I travel, I imagine different ways of being free. I pretend to be a citizen of the world. I make myself up as a common woman, I disappear into the crowds and try to be happy. I cross the streets and talk about anything while I consider life could be that way too, lived not as a personality but as a person. Yes, I seem like a free woman, but I'm not, because Havana is always waiting.

When I travel, I have access to the Internet again. I begin to speak the truth in a normal tone of voice. I can, in fact, shout what I believe . . . Yes, one hour of scrutiny is worth it, in the end, to fly free for a while. Because I know—we all know—I was born in captivity and now it seems I will never know any other way of getting older. My mouth shut, anguished tears falling on an imagined plate of food.

Two, maybe three generations will pass and we Cubans will still be looking over our shoulders.

An hour of control is worth it if, as soon as the plane doors close, you can enjoy the luxury of forty-five days away from the island and its neurosis.

Sometimes, already up in the air, I fear the plane will turn around, come back to earth, and taxi on the tarmac just to leave me there, in front of a battalion of uniformed men.

Deliriously self-referential, that's how I feel.

But I'll meet García Márquez. I'll see his eyes, his hands. I'll be able to read him another way. Maybe I'll understand why I've chosen to write, despite the fact that, because I write, the solitude makes me feel a peculiar annoyance, as if the page is refusing to obey and resists my texts: once written, the ink poisons them, devours them. But I'll meet García Márquez . . . The plane is in the air and I take Gerónimo's hand. Cuba looks so small down there, while it's so big inside me . . . My problems follow me wherever I go. They're like a hat that travels with me; they're a crown.

I'd forgotten that arriving here always gives me intense pleasure. Mexico City keeps you awake, anxious, like a nocturnal animal in the jungle; the stimulus comes from the danger: The risks you run as you navigate the city sharpen your instincts. The wildest smells and the most acute flavors assault your senses.

There's nothing I can do to relieve the sense of insecurity that circulating through these streets produces in me, because my body still holds on to the strange pain of the kidnapping. I'll never walk through this city again without feeling the fragility of being alive. Mexico City hurts me, and seduces me.

I run through the gauntlet of risks. I know I'm trained to survive anywhere, but the dangers in Mexico City make for uneasiness for someone like me, who can smell the gunpowder and can keep the adrenaline pumping and is in perpetual combat. Do Enzo and his friends still live in this city? I don't know. It's the same city, but I now perceive it so differently.

It's only when I get to the airport that I remember Gerónimo is a famous actor. In my country, these things hardly register. People walk by you naturally. Who could be interested in a Hollywood actor when faced with the daily challenge of survival?

We can barely move from one space to another without his being called out, photographed, embraced. Autographs and selfies.

A huge armored truck transports us on the gray highways through this enormous city that always feels alien to me. On the radio, someone sings: "Lie to me again/your bad makes me feel good."

Later, at the St. Regis, the danger seems to mute with the altitude. The silent city seems to be gagged below us, but the danger beats, it beats between the traffic, smoke, and fear of the gray.

Gerónimo hates to turn on the TV and detests the news; after so many people laying claims on him, he values and reveres silence. He loves to hear me sing old Cuban songs, unknown danzones and boleros, but today I keep silent too.

I shower to get rid of Cuba's heat. Sweat and the smells of the tropics stream down my body like rancid makeup. As I leave the bathroom, I see Gerónimo stretched out on the bed's white silk sheets. His naked body is so perfect, I feel I don't deserve it. His sex has been designed for my mouth, and his mouth distills a lust my sex longs for.

I kiss his body in the night's profound silence. He swells and shivers, lengthens, poisons me with pleasure, wets my neck, drips on my thighs. I wrap him up like a raging warrior. I advance on him, flying over the dangerous city. I don't care about breaking the glass. I leap past the fear. I imprison his sex with mine and sink into the sharp sensation that produces such delight in me. He seems like he's asleep but nothing about him is at rest. I pounce and plunge and shudder. Gerónimo throws me against the bed with a treasonous turn and reels me in. He kills me with pleasure, controlling the tension with three fierce thrusts against my matrix; a frenetic and labored spell holds him against my center, punishing him by taking him on an impartible and irreversible route, a one-way trip. Cornered, suffocating, we journey from inside him to inside me, from his limit to mine, until there's no way out but to shatter. Two screams break the night's silence. Two long cries devastate us as we fall on the sheets, that immense combat zone which is the bed splattered with our ardor.

There's a knock on the door. The hotel security fears the worst. I'm experiencing the best of my body pouring into his.

Nude, we open the door. The waiter blushes. We're in Mexico, and there are still norms amid the danger and risk. We offer apologies and order a light dinner.

Silence, kisses, cuddles . . . We put Havana someplace far away and exotic, though ten hours ago that exoticism was our quotidian existence. We fantasize about being in two cities at once as my tongue rescues some of his sweat, which is also mine.

We were trying to get to Fuego Street but the police stopped us. The taxi dropped us off at the entrance to the Pedregal Gardens because it couldn't go any farther. An officer recognizes Gerónimo and tells everybody else he's Spider-Man. I don't recall him ever playing that character but, in the end, it's the code that gets us past the rope. Just a few autographs, two or three photos, and that's it, the way has been opened to us.

The meeting is supposed to be more or less at this time, but it's getting dark. Is it going to rain or is it night? Something's happening. An uncomfortable silence ricochets in the labyrinth of houses that look unoccupied. Perhaps this deep solitude is normal in this neighborhood.

I doubt García Márquez would want to write about Mauricio, about this man whom I can't seem to understand. I don't think we'll find anything, but we're on our way, and very excited.

Gerónimo thinks the story of my presumed father would make an excellent first novel. He asks me to think about it. He says I don't have to stop writing poetry, that I can write in both genres and, of course, I can write the script about what we're researching now. Whenever Gerónimo gets fired up about something, he starts talking in English. I don't understand his other language so I stop listening and it becomes the background music between us.

I promise him I'll write that novel, especially because of how thrilled I am when I think that, in just seconds, I'll be before García Márquez.

"Call him Gabo," says Gerónimo enthusiastically. "That's what he likes to be called."

"I'll call him Gabo," I say, vibrating like an acoustic instrument dying to be played.

We pause for a soft kiss, as if caresses under flowering trees in April were part of the ritual process that awaits us at the end of the street. The neighborhood is very charming, sweet and fanciful with its vines and roof tiles.

"Will we meet Mercedes?" I ask, curious.

"Of course I'll introduce you to Mercedes. You'll love her. She's enigmatic and sharp. There's no meeting without Mercedes. Our meeting isn't for another forty minutes. We're much too early."

"How many more blocks?"

"Walking down from here to there, about four or five more curves."

"What was the first thing of his that you read?"

"*One Hundred Years of Solitude*, of course. And you?"

"A story called 'Eyes of a Blue Dog,' and then I couldn't stop reading him. I was fourteen and I'd escape from school to go to the library at Casa de las Américas to consume it all. *One Hundred Years of Solitude* made me a poet, because that's poetry . . .'"

The voices just beyond the next curve slowly piqued our interest. Two motorcycles with cameras passed between us, separating us; then screams, an ambulance in the distance, reporters, more cameras; the situation was incomprehensible. We inched up to the unknown, which, in some way and from far away, seemed fatal. We walked maybe twenty yards only to realize that . . .

There was an ambulance at the door, where more than three hundred people had gathered to see the precise moment in which the stretcher, duly covered, was slid inside the vehicle.

The reporters were shouting and the cameras wouldn't stop flashing. In the middle of the chaos, a gorgeous woman with downcast eyes reported on the death of Gabriel García Márquez, just as a frightened Gerónimo fled in the opposite direction of the rush of reporters. Once again, I'm abandoned, somebody leaves me in the craziness of a critical and anomalous situation, leaves me alone in a swamp of pain and confusion. It's death again.

My heart stopped in front of the big colonial door at 144 Fuego Street and I said to myself, *I'm always late to what fascinates me* . . . I opened the cage of my body freeing my heartache like yellow butterflies.

This is the end of the fable that connects me to my parents.

I crossed the street dazed by an inconceivable emotion and lost myself in the interminable alleys on Fuego.

11

The story isn't what you want to tell, but what the story
   itself dictates as it reveals itself.

On the screen I watch as the camera pans slowly over an
immense and grayish rice field. The marshy landscape shimmers
in the lens, revealing a balance of burning sun and sky.

Gerónimo and I get up every day before sunrise to meet
with old retired military personnel, ex-combatants from Mauricio's generation, who might have known him.

I stopped going to these meetings, which were practically
interrogations, because their voices and tone reminded me of
the worst of Cuban cinema. There was a false and hyperrealist
feel to it all.

The truth has suffocated them and you never know if lying
is their way of breathing, of lightening their loads, of getting
distance from where they are now.

We divided the work between us. Gerónimo brings home
the images, downloads them to his computer and then to my
laptop in an attempt to keep them from getting lost in case of
another raid. I check the dialogue, add time codes, and disap-

pear. I feel like these testimonies contaminate the little poetry I've managed to recover and conserve.

I touch the glass to wipe away a stain, clean the image with a cloth. They digress. They blink nervously. Do they lie? Yes, many of them lie. Are their consciences at peace? Do they think they did the right thing? Would they do it differently? Would they do it again?

There's a very common script to these meetings.

At the beginning of the conversation, they feel like undefeated heroes and, also, like saints almost, the kind we should talk about in dramatic passages.

But little by little, as the rum takes over, a very disagreeable layer of forbidden stories floats up to the top. A face, a painful grimace, will fill the screen. Then come the declarations, the tortures, the executions and betrayals with which, generally speaking, or so they say today, not one of them was in agreement. The fact is they were participants and the war wounds tattooed on their flesh are the greatest proof. The trembling of their hands. The pain deep in their eyes.

The last interview was at a cattle farm. *How many innocent men could this officer have killed?* I wondered as I paused the image, looking him over, trying to find something lyrical about him, the part of them they all struggle to reveal at the end of the interview: showing photos with their grandkids, poems written while on assignment in the Congo, letters to a lover as they left Colombia with a load of merchandise on a sailboat with a faulty motor nicknamed El Quixote, drifting, and unable to communicate with Havana—"I never knew anything"—and no compass or clue other than being a bulletproof survivor. As I watch each one remembering their "adventures" with such nostalgia—adventures quoted by Régis Debray in certain articles—and which they each show off with certain pride, savoring their sadness and circling an uneasy road of epic weaknesses, exhibiting scars like medals, calling out their guerrilla days, their disembarkment and triumph, I think I do not want to have a father like that.

The speaker is Manuel, alias El Chigüín.

El Chigüín: *I consider myself a warrior. The warrior's soul is represented in various cultures as a butterfly. I drank water from ponds in Africa so the parasites would inure me and I could travel lighter through the trenches (. . .) The day I left on the sailboat from Buenaventura, I didn't realize the storm would toss me back on shore. If I didn't burn it down, they would burn me down.*

He's small and seemingly inoffensive. He speaks with a great deal of satisfaction about his "Cuban Rambo" days. One curious bit is that, in these interviews, no one ever says who gave the orders. The missions appeared out of nowhere? Disembarking, liquidating, attacking, extracting, transferring, or exploiting different zones, rescuing people and materials. Not even when drunk will these guys let on about any kind of hierarchy that could help decipher who gave the divine orders.

Gerónimo: And you, Chigüín, aren't you afraid of talking? Aren't you worried the information you've given me could leak and you could be taken before a military tribunal, or condemned by one?

El Chingüín: First of all, someone who asks me that question would be incapable of giving me away. I chose you because you're ethical, you seem like a strong person who will not let anything intimidate you, and that . . . that is only discovered, learned, and practiced in another type of battle . . . when one has been an intelligence agent.

I spent the wee hours of my mornings inserting codes to identify the immense cast of characters and their clandestine lives. We urgently needed another face to emerge from them, that of Mauricio Rodríguez.

I refused to go with Gerónimo because I've never gotten along with the military world. Soldiers, police officers, agents, all that makes me profoundly depressed. To fix things in life with death strikes me as a crime. I don't know what to do with their pathological lies.

Since they've been denied a role in the history archives, these folks yearn to be protagonists, and the story we start to construct begins to reflect more who they wish they'd been and not so much who they were.

El Chigüín: What should I expect? Death? Yeah, yeah, I played that part too. I also took part in firing squads, and if the opportunity arose again—if there was a grievance—I'd do it again. I'm looking for someone who'll kill me (guffaws). I don't want to die of cancer, that's no way to go for me (nervous smile). (. . .) For example, my experience with Mauricio Rodríguez, everybody knows about it here, but few have the balls to talk about it . . . I was part of the firing squad . . . Mauricio took off his Rolex and gave it to the officer who had escorted him there.

Oh my God! Gerónimo hadn't told me Mauricio had finally come up in conversation. I was so startled that I pressed a button and turned off the computer. It was so strange to have him pop up amid that sad forest that had been surrounding me, almost asphyxiating me.

I tried to get back to the interview to code it but I began to get dizzy. It all threw me back to such a hard reality that, like my parents, I needed to step away from it, edit it, censor it, pull it out of me.

I tried, I took deep breaths and went back to the moment when Mauricio is mentioned.

El Chigüín: Mauricio took off his Rolex and gave it to the officer who had escorted him there . . . El Macho, that's what we called him in the Sierra because he was just a kid when he went up but he had the soul of a man, a real man's man. El Macho took off his watch, which had been a present from the Comandante, and gave it to El Turco. And, just like he'd requested from his cell, he got to direct his own execution. I saw it with these very eyes that'll soon be six feet under. That guy sure had a huge pair of balls, my man. Ready, set, fire! And there he went.

Gerónimo: I always thought Mauricio Rodríguez was just a popular legend.

El Chigüín: It was Che who was a popular legend. El Macho was one of the guys who was there so Che could be a popular legend, and I say Che because he was a foreigner, but I could give you quite a few more names. People, get it through your heads: For there to be a hero and a martyr and a symbol, there has to be an El Macho holding him up. There are no miracles! War isn't some little history book. Every time I see kids at concerts with Che on their shirts, I just wanna . . .

I couldn't take it anymore. I put on a dress, grabbed my

purse, opened the door, and went out for a walk. I needed to rethink if I wanted to continue working on a story like this. I felt dirty, contaminated by things that had nothing to do with me. *Why am I even involved in this?*

I've struggled plenty these last few months with the idea that another person could be my father.

My mind runs away, bolts, refuses to touch all that blood. An alien blood is trying to take over my genes.

Was this the reason why my mother chose not to involve me?

I can't, I just can't with this, I said to myself while walking in Vedado, trying to get some air as I made my way through the familiar streets, labyrinths, passageways that guided me, the same Cleo, the same Cleo I've always been.

As day was dawning, with a *son* playing in my head and the sound of a pair of maracas splitting my skull, I made my way back through the empty and dreary gardens of the Hotel Nacional. With so much rum in my body, and after hours of watching the waters caress, lick, and swallow the city at the end of such an indiscernible spring, besieged by my apprehensions, finally, at four-thirty in the morning, when you can't tell if you're ready for bed or just getting up, I crossed my tiny yard and let myself drop on the colonial-style chair in the vestibule.

In a jasmine mist, neither awake nor asleep, and experiencing the same lethargy from which poetry is born, I could taste the salt of the bay on my lips, reconstruct the landscape in water and India ink, my sad and worn nib pen rendering a blurry view of that cattle ranch where Gerónimo had filmed the interview.

When I opened my eyes, the sun was already out. This was a proper daybreak, and my sense of belonging recognized it as such and took responsibility for the chain of unwitting and sentimental stimuli that streamed under the tiny bridge between dreams and reality. These are my birds, the ones that nest in the awning on my terrace. A little farther off, my neighbor's roosters present themselves, like they do every day. These are my smells, my noise, and even before opening my eyes, my fingers recognized the bruises on the chair where my mother would rock me to sleep during summer night blackouts.

My fears depend on the scale of what I can stand. My apprehensions are the consequences of battles I've been able to fight on my terms. What I can't take is a fear greater than my valor. That's the difference between an artist and a heroine.

Do I really want to risk getting myself dirty? I asked myself from the depths of the nightmare. As a response, I received the sweet salty taste of Márgara's café con leche. She'd come in stealthily, trying not to wake me. She'd come to save me from this exile, baiting me whether I'm asleep or awake.

12

On my body, there are pieces I've worn as armor. A slip, lace, veils, onionskins to hide my soul, see-through hose, layers of silk on skin shield me as I flee, get lost, and then emerge from the deep forests that intimidate me.

Apocryphal stories and secrets settle on my body, which is a map, a vital drawing, to guide me on a lucid tour that travels from feelings to actions and possesses me.

Below my legs—exactly between my belly and your eyes, between laughter and desire, between the smell and taste of us both—is a woman anointed with your balm, the one before you now, naked, taking you, stark, wordless but for her sex.

When we can't talk, when saying everything is doubly difficult, when there are differences in our languages or in our way of feeling or thinking, we let loose with our bodies and lower our guards, burning down the protective circles that previously shielded us. In that blunt and delicious danger, in that contamination of rage and pain—that's where desire truly resides.

Ssshhhhh!

We spent the morning in bed. He had waited for me all night. I couldn't get over the previous night's insomnia. We'd make love, nap, barely utter a word, then sleep again. The day seeped in through the blinds. I tried to will myself up but fatigue knocked me back down on the bed until I was fast asleep.

I wanted to tell Gerónimo I couldn't go on with his project. Where was the poet, the essayist, the writer in me?

I wanted to explain that following those warriors' paths would end up hurling me into their own manure, and I couldn't afford that luxury. I'm alone and have sole responsibility for myself. I gain strength from being alone, from watching out for myself; being my own guard keeps me strong.

Unquestionably, this project isn't for me. I can't deal with it; it's bigger than me.

I closed my eyes as I rehearsed the thousand ways I could convince Gerónimo, but not a single word came out of my mouth. My sex rushed to his sex, trapping it savagely and without explanation.

Márgara brought us lunch in bed: okra and chicken, plantain and corn balls, white rice and fried yams. We made a nest underneath my bed's mosquito net.

"C'mon, get up so I can fix the sheets. You two are like a couple of babies in a crib," said Márgara as she shook the sheets and attempted to make the bed.

By dusk, I knew Gerónimo had spent the better part of his childhood without parents. His mother died first, then his father. He and his little sister ended up in an adoption program for Latino kids. After a very long wait, when they finally found a home, Gerónimo was already too old and he wanted to go someplace else, by himself, to study acting, along with people he'd already chosen along the way.

That dawn I realized what it was like to be aimless. Childhood is the loneliest and most unjust time in our lives. Everyone has a say, authority, and the ability to intervene in our lives.

I was always in a hurry to grow out of childhood but, as some kind of punishment, I seem to be here still, anchored, asking myself questions about it.

I'm trapped, full of doubts. I don't want to consider that my mother betrayed my trust, my integrity.

If I end up proving I'm not the child of the man I thought was my father all these years, if I confirm that my mother preferred to keep a heavy political silence over telling me the truth, if I end up discovering this nightmare is real, then I'll have to start over again, just like Gerónimo.

"Did you also write while your parents were alive?"

"Not that seriously. I wasn't yet aware that this is all I wanted to do."

"Then you've already become something else. You've become an author since they've been gone. Think about everything you've experienced since then."

"Parents are human, and they make mistakes. They tell us they'll be there all our lives, but they can't keep their word forever. They leave us. I feel strange since they've been gone. There are things I still don't understand about their deaths."

"Why don't you go to therapy? They probably have good therapists here."

"Yes, the kind who, when squeezed, will tell all. That's how it is with the *babalawos*. Everything you confess to them ends up with those who you least suspect. I can't risk it."

"Did you ever suspect your family was hiding something?"

"Never. But now I understand why the past was a point

of no return in this house. It was something we never talked about, something we hid from all the time. I always thought to allude to the past was a sin. I never ask anyone about their families, because I was raised to believe that to inquire was bad manners. Now I think I understand some things. All that's left is to confirm them."

I had promised myself I wouldn't so much as glance in the project's direction anymore. I asked Gerónimo to free me from all of it, to forget about finding this person and writing about him.

I knew this would separate us. I knew Gerónimo's time in my life was based, exclusively, on finding my alleged father. He's a practical man who changes depending on the role he plays and, back then, his role as director was the only thing that really mattered. I was part of that.

It took hours for me to explain things to him and it would take even longer to convince him, because no one can understand, like I do, how damaging it is for me to stick my hand in my parents' business; that world is so sordid and black that it swallows me whole, and I don't have the antibodies to protect myself.

Continuing with the past, Gerónimo showed me outtakes from his movies, ones I'd never seen. He screened fragments from the three films he considered the most exceptional of his career. He'd received an Oscar for one of the roles. Gerónimo fell asleep after the third one, which I'd decided to watch in its entirety because I'm enthusiastic about Sandinismo. As I watched him sleep, I thought the actor on the screen was a different person. I fixed his hair, kissed his neck, and slowly uncovered him to see his stupendous naked body.

No, he didn't seem the same person at all. The one resting on my lap was a common man among mortals while, on the screen, the most beautiful man in the world screamed, got high, and suffered deeply while making me cry; he even managed to exasperate me, leaving me powerless.

When I finished the last reel of the third film, still overcome by the images, I became just an average woman and sneakily made love to him. I needed him to stay asleep because that night, while he dozed, and just this once, I could possess the actor instead of the man.

We learned about Chigüín's death at six in the morning. A strange car accident had ended his life.

Alberto came early with the news. He'd heard about it from the veteran's eldest son, with whom he'd attended military school in the Soviet Union.

The three of us had breakfast in silence, knowing his death was no accident.

I decided to accompany Gerónimo because the news had rattled him; Chigüín had been his best witness.

At noon, we arrived at a house in Siboney where peasants had been singing since the wee hours. Chigüín had made it clear: The day he died, he wanted music, and nothing to do with crying or solemn funerals.

The house was very odd; it must have won an architectural prize in its day. I'd never been inside such a gem of a place before. But, from the looks of it, its current inhabitants never quite perceived or understood the soul or personality of this 1970s original. Who was the architect?

Everything inside—the furniture, decor, and even its residents—contradicted the lyrical morphology of the place: rolling glass panels, wide hallways leading to the bedrooms, waterfalls that emptied into a pool surrounded by river stones or close-cropped Asian maidens.

Each room in the house, at each level, was illuminated by skylights that let in the natural sunshine.

Everywhere around us there were crafts, colored photos, political posters, Vietnamese mats and rugs with Moorish land-scapes that served as hangings on the few walls with enough room and without glass tile murals.

This was, without a doubt, a true struggle for spatial domi-nance between two Cuban social classes trying to possess the same building. The bourgeoisie "fled in terror" (that's what we were taught to repeat over and over at school), while the reb-els took over spaces they continue to inhabit without under-standing.

At least, what I could see hadn't been modified; everything looked like it was in good shape. The house's muzzled essence searched for light, vibrated, radiated, and tried to recover its spirit, tried to reach for the sky, like the vines sprouting from the side columns.

I wanted to continue to ponder it all but my predicament was calling me back. I'm going nuts. Everything seems to be about me and my problem. Every gesture, every look, in the faces and greetings of those old warriors seemed to say: The daughter of the Spy—Rodríguez's daughter—The traitor's daughter—The hero's daughter. El Macho's daughter is here. There, along with the guitars and the sad songs, the *décimas* and the peasant laments, I thought I'd found the answer to my drama.

Their wasted faces, their wrinkles, their war scars, their twisted features with unbalanced and mournful smiles drawn with dentures that were too big or too unreal, with sad eyes, complicit grimaces, guilty tics; quiet or restless faces. And there I saw myself, suffering with them. Civilian clothes worn like military uniforms, uniforms chock-full of medals, the escorts alert to whenever something or someone important crossed the threshold.

Alberto moved about that house like a fish in water. He'd brought two bottles of rum, found some glasses in the kitchen, and began to serve everyone. He looked after the combatants, chatted with them, hugged all those veterans who, it seemed, he knew very, very well.

I said something in a quiet whisper to Gerónimo but he thought none of this was unusual.

"This is an island, Cleo. Everybody more or less knows everybody else."

"You don't know what you're talking about. I don't know anyone here."

"But maybe they know you."

"Me? Why would they know me?"

I went out to the patio to get some fresh air. I still wanted to find a plaque with the architect's name. I watched for a while as the chickens laid their eggs under the enormous wooden fence that encircled the mansion.

Since I was little, I've found getting lost in gardens to be a great pleasure. I picked up little blue ceramic squares that had been dispersed and buried in the dirt. I put together a jigsaw puzzle with them and remembered a spur-of-the-moment game about a path to heaven made from rocks we'd spread over puddles where the motley chickens and local ducks would bathe.

In the distance I heard Alberto's voice nervously calling out to me. By this time I'd crawled under the house, with its capricious levels supported by pilings covered with shells, reeds, and green lizards.

"Cleo! Cleo! Where are you? Come here, I want to introduce you to someone."

"I'm here," I said from the humid depths.

"Here where?"

"Beneath the floor . . ."

Alberto came down uneasily on the slabs that made up the steps and found me, under the house, picking up snails of all colors.

"Hurry, come with me," he said, like a boy who's up to some mischief.

We entered through the service door. In the kitchen, the musicians were tuning their guitars, and in the living room, a *décima* singer who sometimes stars on TV was rhyming *revolución* with *son* and *corazón*, *tristeza* with *firmeza*, and *muerte* with *suerte*. The guitars were full of sorrow but flirted around the voices and the poet's whimpers. I let myself go, flying like a ribbon in Alberto's hand.

"And who's this girl?" asked the widow, very upright, next to the coffin.

"This is Cleo, the girl who was helping with your husband's interview, remember?" insisted Alberto. But the widow was confused.

The woman's daughter joined us.

"Mama, she's the American actor's girlfriend," she said, raising her voice so she could be heard. "Alberto just explained to us she's the little girl that . . . she's Aurorita Mirabal's daughter. The doctor."

"Who?"

"The doctor. The one who taught Chacho and me how to swim in Varadero. The one with the big wooden house in front of the water."

"Ah, yes, yes," said the elderly woman. "And did anyone ever tell her she's El Macho's daughter? Your father was very handsome and when your mother . . ."

"Mamáaaaa!" the daughter screamed.

A huge Cuban flag covered the closed coffin. After these outbursts, there was a terse silence, followed by murmurs and coughs; weeping and music from the living room flooded the somber, flower-covered corner where they'd laid out the body.

My own body felt alien. It wasn't obeying me. I wanted to take control and breathe calmly but my legs were trembling and my hands could barely hold on to the glass of rum Alberto had handed me in the confusion of voices and tears. I thought about running, going home alone, but Alberto kept signaling for me to wait a little longer.

Gerónimo was recording everything that was going on. He followed everyone who came in and out of the wake. He followed any little thing that happened, and he wouldn't take his eye off the viewfinder.

I tried to squirrel back behind the house, to retreat underneath it again, but then a platoon of soldiers came in with a floral overlay that read, "For Chigüín, from Comandante en Jefe Fidel Castro Ruz."

The thick smell of the madonna lilies, the constant whispering and the aggrieved looks of the veterans, some of whom we'd already interviewed, paralyzed me. I was just about ready to take off when we heard two shots followed by screams coming from the garden.

"Get out, everybody out! My father didn't have an accident, he was murdered—enough already! Get out of here!" Chigüín's eldest son yelled in both Spanish and Russian. "Out, out all of you! Have the decency to go and leave us in peace."

The young uniformed military officer entered the living room, aiming his firearm toward a median point in the glass. Alberto and I ran. Gerónimo stayed inside, filming. Though we called to him over and over, he didn't respond. I decided to go back in, despite the danger, and grabbed his camera before it dawned on one of the guards to do the same. It was only then he realized it was time to get out of there. As we fled, we witnessed a group of soldiers disarming and handcuffing the young man, who continued to shout insults in Russian.

We gained some distance by picking up our pace and were about three blocks away when we heard one more shot and then some thuds. With our hearts in our throats, we desperately searched for some form of transportation to get out of there, but by this time the police had blocked off the area, making it impossible for any vehicles, much less a taxi, to come in or get out.

The only thing left to do was to walk quietly toward Fifth Avenue, praying for a miracle so they wouldn't take everything Gerónimo had managed to film.

13

By nightfall, we were at Alberto's house enjoying the fruits of his discreet marijuana harvest, which he cultivated himself, dispersed in small hidden pots all over the backyard. Surrendering to the mystic smoke, we flowed, because if we didn't flow from the insanity of it all, the insanity would get to us, would destroy us and tear us to pieces.

Gerónimo, Alberto, and I were stretched on the grass, smoking, laughing without a care, ready for whatever was coming, which, we knew, should be finding my past and accepting it as my present.

Gerónimo recited lines from a famous animated cartoon he'd made very popular by doing voice-overs. We laughed until we couldn't anymore. We were an octopus adrift in the Caribbean, a solitary creature with many hands trying to make ice sculptures at the bottom of the sea, brief sculptures that disappeared each morning with the sun.

In a fit of hope, it occurred to me we could play at telling the truth.

"The truth? Which truth?" asked Alberto, barely conscious; he was the one who had the hardest time disconnecting from the world.

"For example, I could say this is my first time smoking grass," I happily confessed.

"Noooooooo!" they shrieked in unison.

"Also, you are both suspicious of me. I want to help you but you won't let me."

"Suspicion is an illness!" Alberto shouted in his cracked voice.

"Another example: Though it hurts, I'm starting to believe I'm Mauricio's daughter."

"I could say, for example, that we're trapped on this boat and the only one who knows where we're going is you. You know more than you let on, but you throw us off, you throw us off course," said Gerónimo.

"I could say: You don't love Cleo, and that you're only with her to get your hands on the story. I could say she's nothing to you. I've seen the women you're with on American TV," said Alberto between yawns.

"I could say that in this country it's a crime to watch American TV but they let you . . . Why? Because you're an informaaaaaaaant!" I screamed at the top of my lungs.

"I could say I know you have a brother, and I know where he lives," confessed Alberto.

"I could say that if you're giving away all this information, it's because somebody upstairs wants us to have it," Gerónimo said calmly, in a whisper.

"I could say you both talk about me as if I were dead. You exchange information as if I didn't exist. And I'm right here. That's the truth."

"I could say that for the first time you're assuming this is your other life," responded Alberto, surprised.

"I could say that Saturday morning I fucked a black woman who runs a ramshackle grocery, and we did it standing up," said Gerónimo, to ease the tension.

"That's not fair—we agreed to 'tell the truth,'" I protested.

"It's the truth," answered Gerónimo.

"Then tell the whole truth: It was a black man, not a woman," Alberto said, somewhat sarcastically, to correct him.

We cracked up laughing until we went numb. Alberto tried to kiss me but I pushed him away to get to Gerónimo. It was so strange: For an instant, alienated as we were, the three of us shared a kiss.

Hunger, magnified by the effects of the marijuana, invaded my body.

It was time now to get up and walk back to my house, where Márgara always left something prepared in case of emergency. But a greater force seemed to overcome all three of our bodies, consumed by a pathetic autophagy. It just got more and more difficult to stand up, to escape from stupor's embrace and break away from whatever was holding the three of us together.

14

Where it says house, it should say prison.

When we got home, we saw that everything was open—all the doors and windows. Márgara was still waiting for us, nervous, her body bent, reclining on the rocker on the terrace. They wouldn't let her in; they wanted to go over everything without witnesses. This time the raid was accomplished without my presence, but they were still waiting for us.

Márgara's eyes looked like they were out of orbit. She made a bitter gesture I didn't understand, then emphasized it by asking us, Gerónimo and me, to keep quiet, so we did, we kept quiet.

This time they'd left only a few damp papers scattered on the floor. They'd taken every book and notebook from the library, the closets, the wardrobes, the drawers, the shelves, the racks, the trash, and the corner tables.

There weren't very many documents left at the house. We lost a bunch with each raid but this time they'd really outdone themselves. They also took all the cameras, the old cassettes, the DVC, rolls of film, the computers and the video production equipment. But they left Nitza Villapol's recipe book, for which I am very grateful.

Amid all the disruptions, this made some sense because I now understood what they were looking for. Like us, they were all trying to find Mauricio Rodríguez. But there is something about that man that makes him hard to snare; he doesn't bow down, but appears and disappears, escapes and there's no human way of capturing him. We can't do it: not them, not us.

In less than fifteen minutes, a new officer was at the house ever so gently suggesting to Gerónimo that he should leave the country.

"When?" the actor asked.

"Immediately. You're leaving today on the last flight."

"Why?"

"You should know. I haven't been 'instructed' to explain it to you."

When we tried to gather his clothes and pack them in a suitcase, the official, in the kindest tone again, suggested he should leave the country with just his documents and the clothes on his back. They took the camera with the images from the wake as well as all his personal effects. His electric shaver, his pills, his cell phone. None of it would accompany him on his journey out of the country.

When Gerónimo tried to protest, the official explained that they were doing this because of who he was, but if he refused to cooperate, they'd detain him until they could figure out some things they still had doubts about.

"But, detain me for what? I haven't done anything illegal. If somebody's hiding something here, it's you guys."

"Well, sir, it's obvious that what you'd like is to be taken to a detention center, to have some time to reflect and think things through until you can see our point of view. Come with me."

Gerónimo slammed the wall with his fist and it was in that gesture that I saw, for the first time, and only for a few seconds, the man and the actor come together in the same body.

At midnight, I watched them take him out to the street. They didn't handcuff him and they didn't mistreat him, but they expelled him just the same without a right to protest.

Outside, people were watching. It never occurred to me that the people on my block were so aware of our lives.

I could hear his name being whispered. Every minute there were more and more people looking for the actor. It was so strange. Whenever I had walked around with him, I'd had the sense that here nobody knew who he was, or, if they did, that they didn't really care. I remember crossing San Rafael Boulevard, or Neptune Street, taking pictures all over Old Havana, without anyone, except tourists or some of the better informed Cubans, greeting him in any way.

When the car took off, I wanted to chase after it. I walked out to the sidewalk and, when I tried to run up and give him a kiss, two women in civilian clothes whom I didn't know grabbed me and pushed me around until they finally held me by the arms.

"Careful! You little shit!" the taller one screamed at me.

Márgara persuaded them to let me go and they did.

Nobody else did anything. The neighbors retreated little by little and the street was empty in seconds. It was as if nothing had happened.

Márgara closed the whole house; that is, what I still insisted in referring to as a house. It didn't matter anymore if it was open or closed; in any case, I didn't know if I was inside or outside. I fell into her firm, muscular body and broke into sobs, crying until the phone rang and I rushed to it thinking it could be Gerónimo. Instead, it was a correspondent from the international press who needed to interview me and, most importantly, to ask if I knew the whereabouts of the actor. "Who knows?" I said, and disconnected the phone.

Márgara and I crashed on the couch but we couldn't sleep. She got up and prepared me some tea. She came back looking very worried and, as serious as usual, asked me to clear my mind and get some sleep.

"How do you clear your mind, Márgara?"

"By setting aside all those demons you live with, child."

At six in the morning, I was awakened by the sun with the anguish of an incomprehensible feeling that, between dreams, you can't figure out, but stays with you and grows more intense.

Once again, the salty flavor of café con leche, the bittersweet aftertaste dissolving in my mouth.

Once again, raising the altar, although it isn't the real refuge in which to seek shelter. I felt naked and observed in the heart of my house.

That morning, as I looked at the purple tracks left on my arms by the blows I received, the upside-down house, empty, and the beautiful trees in the garden dropping leaves on the terrace, I recalled the amber stain Gerónimo seemed to leave behind when they dragged him to the car that would take him from here. In the moment, I thought maybe he and everything we'd experienced together until that day had just been a bad dream and that, if I chose to share it, few would believe me. There's a big gap between what's real and what's plausible.

I closed my eyes and that amber stain kept coming back time and again. I knew my next book was in that stain.

Then I remembered a poem by Heberto Padilla that I'd read for the first time in Barcelona.

TELL THE TRUTH

At least, tell your truth.
And later
let anything happen:
let them tear your beloved pages,
let them knock your door down with rocks,
let the people
crowd around your body
as if you were
a prodigy or the dead.

My God, that text had come to me like an arrow. I couldn't believe I had learned it by heart.

How long had it been since I'd written anything? I didn't have my computer. I didn't know if they'd give it back to me.

I needed pencil and paper. I went in my bedroom and saw Márgara had placed my mother's old, small computer on the bed—I thought it'd been lost in the first raid—the unmistakable fountain pen with my grandfather's initials (a souvenir from Gerónimo), and a new notebook. Inside I saw only these simple words in Márgara's script: "Write and be quiet."

15

DAZIBAO

Let the masses hate this woman
and let the organisms of the state
break their contacts with her by special decree.
Let her quickly lose her judicial standing
her rights as a citizen
her ration book and her identification card.
Let the folder and the copy of her birth certificate
vanish into the dusty
notebooks of the Municipal Courts.
On this wall I denounce her in front of the people
here I'll expound on how she left one evening
without prior warning without a word
and without love.
I'll inscribe her beauty on this wall
and extinguish, with a suicidal gesture, the light in her eyes
on this wall I'll put out the fire in her mouth and on her body
stretch her long legs
stop the movement of her adolescent pianist hands
and record the complicated world that is her hair.

I'll leave her here so she can be seen
next to this reclamation
this cry against loneliness
this grave social conflict of which only I suffer
and turns me, at least for tonight,
into a dangerous man in the city.
Raúl Rivero

I wouldn't open the door and only occasionally answered the phone. Only the times I'd agreed to with Gerónimo, my agent, and my editors.

I wrote like an automaton. I talked to myself and read aloud each of the fragments of my novel in progress.

I'd erase what I wrote, tore apart pages with drawings, returned to the keyboard, cried, laughed, showered, came back to the writing machine while still dripping wet, ate alone, drank alone. I felt as lonely as a dog abandoned on the highway.

That's how I spent the end of summer and all of fall, though fall is imperceptible here.

Sometimes I'd be visited by two or three officers who'd come to ask me if I was willing to collaborate with a report about the research I had done with Gerónimo. I'd refuse and that, I know, lengthened my confinement.

My only joy had to do with Márgara. I'd anxiously wait for her, for hours, so I could read her everything I'd written overnight. I slept during the day and wrote at night.

As soon as I finished breakfast, I'd go to bed and wake up only to have lunch and look at everything with a fresh eye. I'd compare the revised pages with Márgara and then say goodbye to her, sometimes until the following Monday.

I rarely went out. My weekly outing was to the Immigration Office, where I would ask to have my passport returned and get no answer. I urgently needed to apply for a visa to the United States so I could meet up with Gerónimo in Los Angeles. They were already editing the movie but the Cuban authorities demanded I wait and come back the next month. The letters of invitation would expire and Gerónimo's office got used to sending a new one every two months. By the beginning of December, I was desperate.

"What would you think if I talked to Alberto?" I asked Márgara one afternoon, interrupting our silence and only a half hour after reading to her, for the fourth time, the new version of my book's final chapter.

Alberto had disappeared from our lives the same day as the raid. It might just be my imagination, but I seriously think even he had been caught off guard by everything that happened.

Márgara made a face that suggested she didn't approve, but I let the thought rest in my mind, kept it there all night and, at daybreak, exactly at six when it was getting light, I dialed his number and invited him over for breakfast.

He seemed defeated, thinner, bearded now; his face looked anemic. As always, Márgara made herself scarce and then, without a word about what we both knew, I asked for his help.

His eyes lit up when he realized I was alone, almost dead socially, and that I needed him. He took my hands and promised, in a schmaltzy and almost melodramatic way, to help me get out of here.

"How?" I asked, pulling my hands back, a little alarmed by the excessive tenderness.

"I don't know. I have to get organized, I've been disconnected from everything. They kicked me out of the Party. I'm unemployed. I barely have enough to eat."

"Then come have dinner with us every night. When Márigara leaves, I get very lonely."

"Aren't you writing?" he asked, staring me right in the eyes.

"No," I said firmly, but using my best victim voice.

As soon as I closed the door and saw Márgara's face I knew what would come next. But it didn't matter because that was my only route of escape. I couldn't see any other way.

"Be very careful, child. That man has always been after your bones."

Marijuana creates the illusion of a relationship with whomever I smoke it, a very intense connection. While I am under its spell, it seems to transform me into someone who's dependent on others, a person I'm not and one I'll never be. When my parents died, I learned about the uselessness of emotional dependency. We are profoundly alone, and I'm no exception.

No one has ever—no matter how much love they profess—been able to keep their promise to always be there, eternally, by another person. Not parents, not children, not siblings, not lovers.

I refuse to create connections I'll have to dissolve later. Passion is a straight line to that dependency. I'd rather establish rational relationships that skirt passion and improve on it within a reasonable time.

★

After so much concentration and so many parades, after so much camping, so many bunk beds, after so much overcrowding, here I am, profoundly alone, but addicted to finding others with whom to communicate and share my life.

During these last few evenings, I wait anxiously for Alberto. Havana's few cold days were upon us and during this time another body felt like a treasure.

Who said there are no insufferably cold days in Havana?

The humidity digs into your bones and sneaks into your soul, rattling you.

Stretched out on the couch, with coats on and only a little bit of light in the living room, we smoked and watched movies rented from underground clubs. We ordered pizzas and hamburgers from nearby eateries, reheated Márgara's food, bought beer, listened to music, danced, emptied the bottles and let them accumulate by the patio's entrance.

Sometimes he fell asleep and I stared at him through the light filter pot installs in my eyes. He's not beautiful but he's not ugly either; he's a common man, someone who doesn't seem to want anything from life anymore. He let his beard go for days at a time, like somebody who doesn't care about looking good anymore, or maybe, simply because he couldn't find something to shave with. I asked myself what Alberto would look like if he got cleaned up and ate better. Cubans, generally speaking, are handsome, but that beauty is usually hidden by the effort to resist waste and annihilation. The lyrical features begin to fade, lose their charm, stop being what they once were, vanish and gain greater distance from the pictures on their ID cards, which were taken when they were twenty years old. They become someone else; they age at an impressive rate. They desert themselves, escape, yes, but where do they go?

Could I get used to living with a man like this? No, no, I couldn't. I was adrift but even so, I couldn't take that step. I wasn't desperate. What I really wanted to do, though, was to read Alberto my novel. But I didn't, I contained myself, because something told me I shouldn't, that he wasn't trustworthy. And, besides, I had already told him I wasn't writing.

"Good evening," Alberto said, coming to from his lethargy, getting up slowly to go to the bathroom, and rearranging, to my great surprise, a pistol he had tucked into the back of his pants.

A gun? I'm getting him out of here for good tomorrow.

For me, that was it. The night had ended.

16

When Márgara arrived, I'd already left. For the first time ever, I needed to go to a hotel to get an Internet connection in Havana.

I'd promised myself I'd never do that. To write my password, to let it go through an internal server, to give my privacy away one more time, it's like undressing in the middle of the street, like revealing my writing, risking that it'll be stolen without ever being published. But this time I had no choice.

It was a risk, I knew, but very necessary.

I couldn't have the original manuscript at my house even one more day. A novel isn't meant to be kept hidden in a drawer until someone finds it. A novel needs air, ink, light. It needs to be seen by editors, to go out into the world, to fly.

Alberto's gun was now the secret weapon pursuing me on the streets, the motivation to launch my novel far and beyond.

In a small office in Barcelona, someone was waiting for it.

Márgara and I unpacked everything they'd returned which, of course, wasn't everything.

I felt almost happy. It was like receiving gifts from myself, things I'd sent myself. Like what the tide brings in at dawn and you discover while walking in the early hours on the cold sand.

I was so scared of opening things up and not seeing essential items like photos of my parents, or my computer. What had they returned? What had they kept?

With a knife, Márgara opened the first box. A thick smell of cigarettes and alcohol rose from my belongings.

Slowly, as I began to touch them, I felt they no longer had my scent nor my spirit. They'd been manhandled, used by others. They had an alien film to them and no longer seemed trustworthy. They'd been violated.

I rescued the photos of my parents from the wreck, and the correspondence with my grandparents during their travels.

I now had back my books by Jorge Luis Borges, José Martí, Julio Cortázar, J. D. Salinger. Postcards from my return to Cuba, the photos from when I climbed Pico Turquino with my classmates at the end of twelfth grade. I recovered more than I'd imagined.

I checked the collection of *Lunes de Revolución* magazines, which my mother had treasured. It was weird, but each and every issue had been returned.

I opened my computer and charged it and soon realized there was absolutely nothing on it. Not a single program survived this time around.

One of the boxes was full of correspondence that had arrived at the Havana post office but had never been delivered to me.

One was a letter from my friend Armando in New York. It seemed to have been written before my parents died. I'd never received it. Had he received mine?

Dear Cleo,
Too much silence.

How have you been?

I thought of you today. I spent all afternoon at Epistrophy, an Italian café, my favorite, enjoying being alone in public. It's on Mott Street in Nolita, a lovely little neighborhood near SoHo. You'll see. It was there I wrote part of *New York Isn't You* and *The Book of Brief Loves*, which were published last year in Barcelona. I've saved you copies so I can give them to you when you come here. It's time for you to visit, even if it's just for a few days. I'd love to go out with you the way we do in Havana. I know you're going to love it; you know I know this city like the back of my hand.

The trip back home was very beautiful. To be able to take care of my mother, and to leave her feeling better, and seeing you again, were real treats. You and a few other friends are what still makes that city for me. The return has been tough. This month I could barely pay rent. I'm living very frugally, even more than usual, but this is my reality. To be a poet, as we all know, is to suffer this sweet curse, perhaps more so here than in other places, but New York still continues to be my favorite city. I'm a divided soul, and there may be no cure at this point.

Roberta, the Brazilian girl I was with in Havana, went back ten days ago. She's reconciled with her husband; I haven't seen her again. I've decided to accept her as a gift from Havana and the gods, although I confess I haven't stopped thinking about her. It hurts every day, at every hour. "I'll have to hide or run," as Borges said in "The Threatened One." Do you remember that poem? I read it to you that day we waited for daybreak at the little beach on 16th Street.

You should come in summer, or, if not, in spring, which is beautiful here and people go outside even if it's just to feel their pain. You know, everyone always says I'm so intense, but you and I both know life is a day and then you remember nothing of it. Think about it and let me know, because it's getting late. I want to spoil you the way you spoil me when I'm in Havana.

Don't forget to say hello to your parents. I'm grateful to them for the ride to the airport. It's never easy to say goodbye to Cuba.

Take care of yourself, my dear Cleo, and finish your book, please.

Love always,
Armando

P.S. It's possible an actor friend of mine will come by to ask you some questions for research he's doing for his movie. It's a delicate matter so he'll tell you about it personally.

Did that mean it was Armando who'd sent Gerónimo my way? It's a small world. Why hadn't Gerónimo told me he was a friend of Armando's? Maybe he assumed I was waiting for him. How long had this research been going on? Anyway, it was impossible to know now.

I discovered messages from friends and acquaintances that had never reached me or my parents. Some were opened envelopes, some still sealed, others sealed for a second time with tape over huge rips. Invitations to conferences, catalogues with scientific bibliographies, postcards from colleagues written in Russian and German.

Some letters wished us a happy new year and others announced weddings, births, the deaths of dear friends.

The vast majority were long apologies to my parents, condolences, lamentations with complex and unanswerable questions about the nature of the fateful accident.

What have I read and what have I not read of all that was sent to me? Who writes to me without my knowing? Why do they let some letters through and not others? Why now?

I asked myself all this as I came back to the universe of prohibitions and returns, where the only thing that wasn't returned to me were the books I'd covered up because they were "prohibited."

At dusk, when Alberto arrived, I realized he was stunned to see my belongings back in their place. Because of his surprise and the caution in his questions, I knew he'd had nothing to do with their return.

I have a terrible defect, which is that I can't shut up when I need to find out something.

"I imagine you had a lot to do with the return of my things, right?" I said, a little sarcastically.

"Me? Well, yes and no."

"So tell me, yes or no?" I insisted.

"There are things a person can't talk about. When did they arrive?"

"Oh, you don't know when they arrived? This morning," I

explained, being very careful. "Three military officers came in a truck. They asked me to sign something then unpacked seven boxes and brought them in."

"This all has to do with a very special request I made but, you understand, I can't talk about that, baby," he explained as he walked over to the kitchen with a bottle of rum he'd brought.

That was odd, because it's always been me who bought the liquor. An armed man drinking rum strikes me as very dangerous. There was no one else here but me and now that I knew about the gun I couldn't stop thinking about it.

I spent the evening trying not to drink. I'd sip a little, then get some ice and try not to lose control. I didn't like the expression on Alberto's face when he came in and saw my things were back. I was trying to figure out if he still had the gun but he had his coat on and he was well swaddled, so I couldn't see anything.

We watched two movies and ate a chicken Márgara had left for us.

He drank and drank compulsively until he finished the bottle he'd brought. He asked for more, whatever was in my cupboard, but I asked him to go so I could rest.

He resisted, demanded I get him another drink, then another. I finally convinced him to leave, that I was exhausted and a little worried. I escorted him to the living room to make sure he'd go but when I tried to push him out, he cornered me against the wall and tried to kiss me. I pushed him back forcefully and managed to land him right at the door. He stopped it from shutting by sticking his foot right between the door and the frame.

"Cleo, c'mon. Open up, open the door," he whispered carefully.

"Please go."

"I have something important to tell you," he said, his hands on the lock, not giving up the little space between us.

"Tell me," I said, opening the door, stepping out.

Alberto grabbed my face with both hands and kissed my mouth. I remained still, breathed deeply, and when he was most relaxed, I gestured as if to let him back in, but then pulled back, closed the door, double-locked it, and quickly walked down the hall until I reached the bathroom.

"Cleo . . . Cleo . . . open the door," yelled Alberto from outside.

I knew all this would happen, Márgara had warned me. I was alone, it was deep in the wee hours and I could hear him shouting even from the farthest part of the house.

I shut myself in the bathroom to take a hot shower and relax my nerves a bit. I needed to sleep. When I stopped hearing his voice, I walked naked out of the shower; it seemed the commotion had passed. *I'll talk to him tomorrow,* I thought, *and maybe if I'm careful, and without alcohol between us, he'll understand.*

I fixed the bed to get in it, stretched my toes, turned off the light, and, just as I was about to close my eyes, I heard two gunshots from the terrace.

In less than five minutes, the street was filled with police.

17

December 17 is a very important day for religious Cubans. St. Lazarus is celebrated and venerated; in the Yoruba religion, he's known as Orula. Many people travel to El Rincón, bringing offerings or dragging their sickly legs, kneeling, walking backward, or simply struggling through each kilometer on foot to revere the miraculous saint encircled by dogs, healer of the sick, guide on the darkest of paths.

Márgara is a devotee of St. Lazarus, that's why she hadn't come to work. My plan had been to meet up with her and get lost in the multitude of pilgrims but I thought better of it. It's much too far and to arrive on the seventeenth itself would be complicated.

There was a knock on the front door while I was in the shower. I tried to hurry but when I opened it there was no one there. I searched the terrace and the garden while still soaped up, wrapped in Gerónimo's gigantic robe. On the sidewalk, I saw a slender young man walking away, slowly, as if he was just strolling by. He was headed toward 23rd Street. He was tall, dressed in blue, and had a package in his hands. I don't know why, even though I was so suspicious, something made me run and catch up to him.

I moved quickly and cut him off, barefoot and dripping. "Hi, good morning, was it you who just knocked on my door?"

"Cleo?" the young man asked, but he was pretty sure it was me, and he looked delighted. "I'm Rubén Gallo. A pleasure to meet you," he said as he shook my hand and spun me, happily, transforming my slovenly robe into a queen's cloak.

"I didn't know you were coming. You've come on behalf of . . . ?" I asked anxiously, wanting to trust him.

"Gerónimo," he said with aplomb.

"Oh yes, then, well, come in, come in. Would you like some coffee?" I asked, urgently wanting to get back in the house.

Rubén is a professor at Princeton and would be coming back to Havana in February, but with his students, who are interested in contemporary literature that distills life in Cuba. When he talked, he seemed completely clean, like nothing bad had ever happened to him. He skillfully hid his intelligence; he struck me as one of those people who doesn't like to show off what he knows.

"You're a friend of Gerónimo's?"

"I met him three weeks ago in New York because he's going to play Proust in a movie and I wrote a book about Proust's Latino connections. We've seen a lot of each other in the last few days. He asked me to bring you this," he explained, extending the package to me. "Please don't put sugar in my coffee."

"Everybody drinks very sweet coffee here, but I don't," I said, serving the coffee in cups that used to belong to my grandparents in Varadero, with the family's initials and a marina in the background. As I poured, I realized how much Cubans (and certainly this Cuban) enjoy showing the leftovers of their ancestry.

"I love your house. What year was it built?"

"It was built in 1935. I adore it."

"Were you born here?"

"I think so," I said, laughing, and infecting him a little with the kind of laugh that has a good share of information . . .

"I understand. This city is incredible, interminable. You get lost . . . Can I see the backyard?" he asked very carefully.

"Yes, of course. Please, make yourself at home."

As I said this, I wondered, *How can I open my house to a complete stranger when I don't trust eighty percent of the people I see on a daily basis?*

I took a knife and opened the package. Inside were two bars of white chocolate, a can of foie gras, and a sealed envelope. I tore open the envelope and inside it was a certified copy of my birth certificate, saying I'd been born in Washington, D.C. There was my name, and my date of birth, but I appeared as the daughter of Aurora de la Caridad Mirabal Álvarez and Mauricio Antonio Rodríguez.

"What I love about the yard are the tiny sculptural ruins that get lost amid the trees. Have you tried to restore them?" Rubén asked from the kitchen.

"Restore them? I don't even remember them anymore . . ."

I broke into sobs, inconsolable now that I was faced with that piece of paper. Rubén came running. I handed him the document and he read it but couldn't say much.

"Well, Cleo, what a moment to meet you, no?"

"Yes," I said, trying to brighten up and even laugh. "It's a strange beginning."

"No, it's excellent. Let's go out for a bit. Do you want to change or do you usually go out barefoot?"

I know it may seem absurd but we hugged like old friends and, of course, decided to go for a stroll through Havana. At this point, there wasn't much to do in the house and I liked the idea of showing Rubén the city.

Before we left, we looked for a good place in the house to hide my birth certificate, which ended up being the refrigerator, between the greens Márgara had washed.

We went on foot from Vedado to Centro Habana. On cool days, it's very pleasant to walk, to saunter around the neighborhoods, to glance inside the houses. Here, the front doors are almost always open and every time you turn a corner, you see the sea. I think of it as a really good joke on the part of the urban planners. I'm of the opinion Centro Habana has been completely forgotten, and won't be restored because they don't think it's as valuable as other parts of the city. But if you look at the art deco buildings, you realize the regular collapsing of buildings around here is a real crime.

"I go out so rarely."

"How can you live here and miss out on all this?"

"Believe me, it's more than enough with what happens just between my four walls."

Rubén and I let bodies pass between us, people who separated us coming and going like automatons on the sidewalk: bare torsos, backs decorated with scandalous colors, loose hair, sensual faces who gazed at us penetratingly, defying us, stomping as we passed by, roughly grazing our hands, rattling us with their voices, imposing themselves on us in the crowd, popping out of Old Havana's interminable alleys, bathing us in a reality that possessed us from head to toe. Drums, babies' cries, laughter, a school choir, bad words and good words, cars trying to start, motors whose growls vanished in the distance, reggaeton, news blaring at full volume, a phone ringing incessantly. Somebody asking for directions with a different accent, and street criers, because now we have street criers again in Havana.

It smells of urban gas here, of fried foods and petroleum, of creolin for mopping, of a whore's perfume blended with the waft of guava pastries; it stinks of sewage, tar, swampland, like the north coast, all stirred up.

It tastes of salt, of a bruised lip.

Rubén and I discovered they were hauling out TVs on several corners. Businesses, bodegas, auto shops would turn up the volume and open the doors so everyone could come in and watch. Somebody was going to talk to the people because, obviously, something serious had happened. The crowds gathered before the screens. The silence was a contrast to the typical rabble of the city. It was almost noon and Cuban TV's theme echoed in the buildings, off the balconies, and down the alleys to the sea.

Stealthily, Rubén and I leaned toward a set broadcasting a science program. And then minutes later, a brusque announcement declared there would be words from Raúl Castro and Barack Obama. Both presidents began to speak at the same time from their parallel realities. The TVs broadcast both versions. Obama was speaking directly, without intermediaries, to the Cuban people. It was the first time an American president looked us in the eye to talk to us.

Raúl explained his reasons for such a step and people looked at each other warily, afraid none of this was real, that we were all delirious, or that it was a trap, another trap life was putting in front of us for us to overcome as Cubans. The bipolarity of the moment, after almost six decades of waiting, the fear of expressing an ecstasy buried for so many years, put us in a strange timeless place, incredulous and alienated. Then, in Cuban code, Obama said, *No es fácil**, and people clapped, recognizing our own words; they hugged, laughed, and started to consider it might be real after all, that things might really change this time.

But in spite of the restrained, emotive, and delicious jubilation on the streets, everything remains exactly the same. The changes will come slowly, I know, but it'll be decades before this reality, the one I've lived without missing a single chapter, will ever change colors.

On the street, we ran into a blond and slender young man with light eyes, who, like us, was happily baffled by the mess of hugs, questions and answers, and so he joined our journey. He was a tailor. He was thinking about maybe opening up a shop in Havana, for suits. How beautiful that would be, we said, celebrating the stranger's idea.

We returned to Vedado and sat looking out at the sea so we could watch the sun go down between the cannons and the gardens at the Hotel Nacional. It was then we realized Cuba had already changed, because people had begun to think about leaders in a more expansive way. Someone else was saying, simultaneously, that there was an option other than immolating ourselves.

Then Rubén started telling how he planned to bring his Princeton students. He told me about Reinaldo Arenas's days there.

"Would you like to give a lecture at Princeton?"

---

* It's not easy.

I closed my eyes and went over the day's definitive events. Change comes all at once, unexpectedly. I remembered a verse by Eliseo Alberto Diego that goes: "If a minute is enough to die, how can it not be enough to change your life?"

Rubén walked me home. We went down 21st Street, stepping on the red bulbs fallen from the trees in Vedado. One of the effects of white wine is to fuse feelings with reality.

A conga line coming from El Rincón, with people dressed in purple as a tribute to St. Lazarus, crossed in front of us. We got caught up in the euphoria and the lyrics of the song: "Obama, Obama, tú sí haces lo que a ti te da la gana."*

When I was about to pull out my keys, I noticed the door was ajar. Rubén looked at me fearfully.

"Don't worry, that's par for the course," I told him. "Good night, Rubén."

"Will we see each other in New York?"

---

* "Obama, Obama, you really do whatever you want to do."

18

I arrive in New York with a temporary exit permit on my Cuban passport, a new American passport, and no idea about what's being said around me, because I'm part of the generation that learned Russian, not English. The words are part of the soundtrack of this new life I needed to start before I dissolved into nothingness, disappeared, died from inactivity while writing, thinking, enclosed, going crazy between my four walls, afraid of leaving the house and getting run over by a car.

If I went out, they'd raid the house and take my travel documents. If I went out, I could have an accident like my parents.

I declared myself sick. I was sick; I'm still sick; it's very difficult to not get sick after all this.

I spent the entire end of the year in bed, depressed, crying, and taking pills Márgara brought me, since she knows so much about psychotropic drugs. Most Cuban women take diazepam, nitrazepam, meprobamate because, as she says, "Life is too hard to go through it with a clear mind."

I resisted as best I could, until I managed to leave Cuba. Getting my American passport, because it had a different surname, became a long paper chase: getting all the documents to get the passport; being watched all the time; dealing with my doubts and my fears. The Interests Section is a difficult passage, a labyrinth you enter without your cell phone, your personal items. I'd been able to get around the long lines because, in the end, I was born in the United States and that gave me certain rights.

I decided I had to be one or the other Cleopatra, the one born in Washington, D.C., or the one who could have been born in Havana. I could contradict or betray my mother, and the path she left outlined for me. I had to stop and consider whether this exit was definitive for me. What has been definitive in my life?

To go to New York to, at long last, jump into Gerónimo's arms has been a suicidal act, embracing the void, like leaping into a chasm without a safety net, the down bed I was hoping to find at the end of my flight.

I arrive in New York to discover this is an abstract place where no one is really waiting for me, where I'm not important, where I don't exist; that's terrifying.

I perceive the distance, the incredible distance, between bodies here, the voices tuned to a different register, such overwhelming times, the curt indifference which freezes strangers when they collide by accident at the subway exit. Where is everyone going? Why are they running? Have they been ordered to be okay? Are they all really okay all the time? *Great! Fine!* Who are they smiling at if they don't know me? Why do they leave me behind as thousands of other similar beings appear and disappear, pursued by the demons of their own objectives?

A city isn't a name, it's not the idea of utopia that others have been able to conquer. It's not an eternal promenade through rarely lit museums. A city, for me, is an exact address to go to, a body to embrace, a dinner to share, a wine to uncork, and a view

that can be understood through eyes that translate the reality
that the body has entered. You don't live somewhere because
it's fashionable or because it sounds refined to live there. You
live somewhere because that's where you work, because you've
found a piece of yourself you want to conquer and adapt to your
image, your energy, your character.

My spirit is still held captive in Havana. I hadn't yet arrived
with my entire being.

You need distance to know yourself, distance to set a date
and meet in order to coincide, distance to send a cautious text
for that very purpose without expressing too much interest.
Distance to love, to feign indifference in being with that person
who'll flee the minute you overcome the distance. A distance
that is reinforced precisely when you try to look it straight in
the eye and tame its remoteness.

"Maybe it's too late for me. Too late in Cuba and too late in
New York; I'm finished. They've beaten me. People like me are
so fragile, we break halfway down the path. We're only good
for writing. Reality kills us, turns us into ink and text, just like
that," I said when I met with Armando at Epistrophy, feeling
his presence like oxygen reaching me at the bottom of the sea
when it seemed like water would finally fill my lungs. At least I
managed to hug him and cry.

"You're tragic and provincial, so weak it's scary, but you'll
deal with this. I love you for who you are, because you're
authentic, not because of your talent. In fact, I don't think you
realize how talented you are. I don't need to do a tarot reading
to tell you what your professional future is going to be."

"Armando, listen, I don't even . . ." I said, trying to explain.

"No. Silence. You need to listen to me. I love Cleo, the one who lost her parents and almost seemed to lose herself, the one who changes surnames and feels hurt by it, the one who took a chance because she thought someone was waiting for her here and then discovered the hard truth. I admire you because you're a naïve survivor, because, in essence, you're a good person who doesn't cease being a good person no matter how many trials are put before her. You fight to continue to believe all that you feel, you get in fistfights with reality, defending your own ideas about consistency and that, these days, is a tough thing to watch."

We paused to taste our coffees and sandwiches, but I could only drink my coffee: a knot between my throat and my belly made it impossible to swallow. The steam from the coffee touched my face. I hadn't even noticed how cold I was.

"I don't like this city," I said, looking out the window.

"New York isn't you; Havana is you, and, look, look how much it hurts you. You're a part of it, don't deny it," he said, smiling with a sweet irony.

"No, I don't deny it. That's why my departure isn't set in stone. What's strange is to realize no one there wants me, no one waits for me," I said, starting to cry.

"Except Havana itself," Armando said, his brow furrowed.

"But an abstract place doesn't wait for anyone, and that's what's happening with New York. In Havana at least I have my—"

"You don't have anything in Havana either. You only have yourself," he said, interrupting my speech and picking up the check.

★

Armando took my bags to his place. He got me out of the hotel where I'd paid for one night and cooked up a delicious plate of Cuban-style shrimp stew and white rice.

I took a hot shower, put on a pair of beautiful warm PJs some old lover of his had left behind in that little Cuban nest in Brooklyn, and allowed myself to have dinner.

After three glasses of wine, when the January cold had finally left my body, I looked at the paintings by Cuban artists he'd brought to New York with him. I'd seen these same pieces in his old place in Nuevo Vedado but here they looked different. I strolled through their textures, I examined the Cuban light that still flickered in my eyes, I imagined the drafts before the paintings, those you can guess at even when the artist tries to bury them under a thick brushstroke; they still leave a trace. I cuddled up on the couch, under the blankets and next to the fire, so I could finally tell him what happened when I arrived in the city yesterday.

I'd changed my surnames, I'd dug into my parents' past, which was also my past. I'd gone down a deep dark hole investigating something which in Cuba is more than taboo. I burned all my bridges because I had made Gerónimo's project my project; his narrative was about my life; I kept my silence, I resisted with great fidelity . . .

"And now? What happened?" asked Armando.

I tried to retell every word and reproduce every expression exactly as it happened, without taking creative license. I wanted this poet to be my witness. I felt very confused about everything and I needed to hear what he thought.

I came on one of those direct flights, full of Cubans who make you feel like you haven't left Cuba until you land and leave the airport, only to recover from that kind of tropical hyperrealism once you hit the streets.

Lidia, Gerónimo's assistant, was there to pick me up and handed me the phone I have now.

"Why didn't Gerónimo come to get me?" I asked her.

"Because Gerónimo in an airport is like a time bomb. The reporters who live and die here wouldn't let us take a step. You'd be in all the afternoon papers, and you don't want that, right, Cleo?" Lidia asked with a look that puzzled me.

I arrived at Gerónimo's apartment and he gave me a distant and icy embrace. I gave him a box of Romeo y Julieta cigars and two bottles of Havana Club rum. He opened the cigars, chose one, tasted it, fired it up, and served himself a good glass of rum on ice. It was eleven in the morning. He moved with a certain gravity, transporting his body's weight in a way that had nothing to do with the lightness I remembered.

I didn't recognize the person who was waiting for me, I didn't know that man. I would have never taken a single step for someone like that; he didn't look like someone with whom I'd have a relationship, with whom I'd share my house, my body, my poetry.

"You seem strange. Is there something going on I don't know about?" I said, unpacking.

"Yes, sit down, Cleo. We need to talk." He paused, served himself a bit more rum, savored the cigar, took a deep breath, and came out with a classic line, "I'm confused."

It's well known that when a man says "I'm confused" it means "this is over." But, in his case, I felt like nothing had ever really started, because he talked to me with cruelty, harshly, as if he couldn't tell how he was hurting me inside and out.

I felt as though the months we'd lived together in Cuba had become fiction, a role he felt obliged to play. He'd made me a character from an animated story who had shown up at his house to reclaim a fantasy. I was that singular creature who'd shown up to say, "Hello, Gerónimo, here I am, your cartoon girl-friend." Then he had to bother to explain to me that I'm unreal, that what's authentic is the nightmare that is his current life.

"That's just a perception," said Armando. "Tell me what he said exactly."

"First, he said I couldn't talk about it with anybody else. He said that several times."

"Yes, but go on," a nervous Armando pleaded.

He explained he was in a long divorce process, that his ex was asking for everything. She'd accused him of domestic violence and was trying to deny him custody of his daughter. He'd never said a word about any of this before.

"Everyone knew but you," Armando said.

Later he told me he was seeing a woman he had talked to me about. In Cuba, he'd referred to her as the "Sociopath." She'd follow him everywhere; she'd even managed to get him on the phone at my place and at the hotel in Mexico. He told me, as if it wouldn't hurt me, as if I were his little sister, that his physical relationship with her was so complex that he could never abandon her. He knew it wouldn't end well, even if he'd gotten another judge, but his weakness for her, what he felt sexually whenever they fought or fucked, wouldn't let him leave her.

"Then why did you ask me to come?" I asked, feeling overwhelmed by all this chaos.

"Because these are things you talk about face-to-face. Because I need you to legitimize this film. Remember that we have a project together. Because it's good for you to get out of Cuba. Because I want to reciprocate what you did for me in Cuba. Because it's important to end things well," he said, very calmly, without any resentment, all the while blowing smoke rings all around the room from his Havana cigar. "You can make yourself comfortable anywhere, in any room except that one, because that one is mine," he said, pointing to his right as he stretched out on the couch.

I grabbed my bags and dragged them through the apartment. The sound of the wheels on the floor, the smell of the cigar, and the lack of food gave me a feeling of nausea, dizziness. I struggled not to faint. I felt awful.

Gerónimo assumed I would settle into one of his rooms. Instead, I turned toward the front door and tried to open it but couldn't. I insisted, turning the key until Lidia came and asked me not to go, that he'd take care of all my expenses until we went to Cannes in May. I listened, then I begged her to open the door. She asked me to please not talk about any of this with the media or any of my friends. I asked her once more to open the door. She did. I took the elevator down and went to look for a hotel.

"Why am I not surprised?" said Armando as he poured himself a glass of cognac.

I walked around New York and saw Gerónimo on billboards advertising an Armani suit.

He was everywhere, including the movies I'd find when searching the long list of TV channels available to me.

It was strange, in every film Gerónimo was a different person than the one I'd known. The person I'd lived with had disappeared, or perhaps I'd invented him. I'm a specialist when it comes to inventing people, things, worlds.

I tried to contact Rubén so I could go to Princeton but he wrote to say he was already in Havana, having a wonderful time and teaching his class.

I began to write a new poetry book that talked about contexts, wardrobes, suits for a man that changed with each story, while Armando coached a French actor who was playing a Cuban dancer. It was very amusing to see the actor in makeup, disguising his voice, his gestures, with something that for us is so natural, genuine, common, and everyday: *cubanía*.

Truth be told, Armando cooked like the gods but sometimes, for the sake of variety, we'd eat out at a Korean restaurant on Grand Street, very close to the apartment, called Dokebi. Since I'm not as interested in actually eating as I am in the spectacle of dining, I'd always choose a dish that required we cook our own meat and vegetables at the table, which had little gas burners in the center.

Other times we'd go to Tabaré, a very good Uruguayan restaurant. The owners are friends of Armando's, it's in the neighborhood, right there on South 1st Street, and they have great meats and marvelous empanadas.

I'd spend hours alone walking around Williamsburg, window-shopping at stationery stores and playing a game of trying to find bookstores with Spanish-language books. What am I looking for here? The days passed without mystery. Nothing was happening, nothing but life. Is there something else waiting for me or is this the end to all possible ends?

19

My father's face appeared in the Moviola; at age twenty his features so resembled mine. The smell of burnt film and Gerónimo's intense scent by my side provoked a brief disorientation, followed by a spasm, almost a lurch in my stomach; but I contained myself, I kept it together until the archival footage was over and the lights came on.

I avoided running into Gerónimo, and when I met him out of necessity, I didn't look him in the eye. I responded monosyllabically and refused his invitations or meetings if they didn't have to do with the film. I wanted to know how I'd come across in the documentary script, because the story belongs to who tells it, and I didn't want to take my eye off its collimator.

They needed to interview me, but what could I say? I was still not used to being the daughter of someone unknown to me, a stranger, a hero, a bandit familiar only to Cuban Intelligence, the CIA, the State Department, an urban legend in whom everything was magnified and distorted.

There I was, blathering before the camera, struggling with the past that was waiting for me. Gerónimo sat in front of me and shot three questions my way.

"When did you know Mauricio was your father? What did

it mean to you once you knew? What does it mean to you to know you're American and that your father was executed the same year you were born?"

I responded with the theatricality he expected. I gave him back his role of hero, which he needed in order to be the great discoverer of the truth.

I cried at the end, and that guaranteed a little drama for the credits. He'd already filmed me walking around Havana and what I was doing now fit perfectly with what he'd already captured. The music he had me listen to would help sharpen the sentiment, emphasizing the melodrama, making even the most stoic cry.

"It was very difficult for me to look at myself in the mirror and see another face, but at least now I know where I come from," I said, figuring we were at the end of the interview. I said it with all sincerity, because since I've discovered Mauricio Rodríguez is my father, it's very hard for me to walk by a mirror. Now I see something in me that I don't recognize.

There was applause in the studio. I'd done the right thing. I expected to see a little of the fiction he'd filmed when he first arrived in Havana with a head full of fresh ideas. This was an experimental film in which Gerónimo played my father, reimagining everything he hadn't been able to figure out. I trusted it could be interesting to work with the apocryphal, but I hadn't been able to preview it. Every day, they'd tell me to wait until the next day, when it would be ready with subtitles.

I met Miguel the last time I was in the editing room.

Who is Miguel? Why was he being interviewed?

I listened to his testimony, and it was so intense I couldn't leave the studio until he finished. Every one of us has a book to write, that's the only way to beat the silence to which Cuba confines recent history.

Miguel is the son of a very famous spy, someone we all knew in the seventies and eighties, thanks to a TV series that ran during the summers on Cuba's two channels. He had infiltrated the ranks of the enemy, reporting each step, every plan, and had been transformed into a hero. But it seemed his real identity was a secret, and Miguel's entire childhood was based on that idea, which was rescued by his mother, who was sharp and naturally warm. Even though the character's name had been changed, and the story was treated as fiction, Miguel explained that the last few times he'd been to Havana, he felt people calling him, in low and feigned whispers, the "spy's son."

Miguel's case is exactly the opposite of mine. He'd had an excellent relationship with his father but lived trying to escape the stigma. I grew up not knowing mine, but it seems fate ran and ran after me until it caught up with me. Today, Miguel is an excellent journalist and edits a magazine dedicated to the visual arts. He was completely up to speed on everything going on in the city in terms of exhibitions and public performances.

It was with him and his friend Olatz that I first went to MoMA on that early morning.

20

MoMA looked like a deserted skating rink. The paintings were reflected on the polished floors. A deep silence surrounded you when standing before them.

It was deep into the night yet there we were.

Olatz had been a very famous model in Paris in the 1980s, and had, for decades, been painted by Julian Schnabel, the father of her children.

An exhibition would be opening the next day about contemporary muses and it was impossible not to gaze upon the three enormous canvases the artist had dedicated to her.

Schnabel's work seemed to pop, to pour out of the frames. I trembled, shook like a leaf when I watched Olatz inspect the lights under which her body would be draped and exhibited for the next few months. Olatz had loaned the pieces so they could be shared with the curious who, during normal business hours, would come see her pose with her back to New York, in front of the studio she had built next to the artist, and with eyes wide open before the landscape of her native San Sebastián.

A silver rain of questions was digging into my skin as I looked at the artwork and the model operating on such different planes. The light vibrated, shook, adjusted, focused on the sublime creature for whom a monument had been erected. Then the connection dissolved and there it was: art, posterity, literary material. How can these pieces connect without the pain of the past? Is there some kind of agreement about how to redeem that past and then leap, unscarred, to the other side of art? Olatz was alive, as was the artwork. They both survived that love. That must mean I have a chance to survive as well. *Maybe I'm just here to understand that,* I thought, breathing in the still moist texture of the curving paint turned into waves between narratives on the solemn canvas.

This was the only hour when Miguel and Olatz could come in peace to the museum so there was no other option but to open it for them . . . and for me. What luck!

Using his charms, Miguel managed to get the museum guards to let me quickly look around the adjoining rooms. That's how I saw—in the blink of an eye—works by Andy Warhol, Jean-Michel Basquiat, Marcel Duchamp, Mark Rothko, and Wifredo Lam.

You don't have to smoke or drink to enjoy kaleidoscopic visions; you don't have to leave your body to feel overwhelmed by the material.

Olatz's green eyes roamed the museum ceiling and I felt my father's face drape over me. My body was a sled Gerónimo had thrown on the bed in my house in Vedado. Cameras followed us again, and I, I was just a stranger, an intruder in the closed museum cage, a spy once more, but a spy at MoMA.

It snowed that day in New York. We went in and out of stores and restaurants that opened early, ate very little, and walked a lot.

"Why do you live here?" I asked Miguel.

"Because it's the only city in the world that lets me have Thai soup at four in the morning and buy a computer at two. Because I can get the newspaper before dawn and see the reviews before I go to sleep. Nothing ever closes here for renovations," Miguel said with that splendid smile as he paraphrased Reinaldo Arenas.

By daybreak, we were still together, now at Olatz's house, where we'd gone from red wine to café con leche with ease, and there, alongside Julian's drama, I swore to not believe in anything but friends ever again. Love passes, the euphoria that provokes desire passes, you can be erased from a photograph by drowning, choking on a sea of India ink distilled by the most absurd passions, you can be exposed and you can be tried, they can dynamite your life, take you and invade you and later claim not to know you; but friendship, that really can last forever.

WHAT IS WINTER

for Miguel
I can't quote
I never quote
The readings travel hidden and in the light inside my
    garments
silk cut on the body Olatz's hand haute
couture in flames
Nobody knows about them they're the silence of my
childhood breath
or they're shown in the revealing intimacy
under the neon of the year's first fire
we were the classics
stretched under the sacred fabrics of

the contemporaries
we read life from memory believed in
the eternity of affections
In parental immortality the wish and miracle
of the cold
That instant when the beauty of the work is brighter
than your word
Your word radiates like those of cummings Your hands
smaller than rain the spasms
of a fearsome winter
January's everyday fireplace and New York
out there like a taxi
The meter still running running running
Life like a song transports itself
in the marvel that is wine
Essential cloaks eternal loves
What is winter?
Pink boots as a gift your laughter like an
individual exorcism and six photos of the yard
stripped of desire
Everything about our winters then was
predictable
I'd already learned that next year we'd be the
same
Washing our hands at a store that sold
Egyptian soaps
The cold would reappear like those poems we
recite from memory
But I can't quote

I don't quote
I punish the body: remember remember remember but
forget
Please forget a little go on
try to forget this.

21

I spent more time on Lafayette with Armando trying on his fantastic gray suit than I did deciding, with Miguel and Olatz, what I'd wear to walk down the red carpet for the film's premiere. I don't really pay that much attention to my clothes, but the Dior dress Olatz chose for me made me feel beautiful: violet, velvet, it uplifted and exalted me. Perhaps it's something my body needed at the time.

What most throws me are the contrasts, from a raid to an interview to a red carpet. Who can understand my life? No half-measures for me, the extremes have always been and will always be where I'm most at home.

I've noticed that, when I'm not at the highest end of a risky enterprise, I can't find my comfort zone. I suffer from a kind of hyperactivity that demands danger so I can use my powers. There's no longer any doubt: I'm a warrior's daughter. My blood carries a kind of clandestine restlessness, a tense nerve that won't allow me to quiet down or leaven my spirit.

We arrived in Cannes after a brief stay in Paris.

Paris is the only city where I feel fine by myself. It's full of secret tunnels that provoke such subtle emotions that I still haven't quite figured them out, personal passageways, involuntary reactions, visceral gestures project themselves on unknown experiences and wait for me at the other end of my life, on the other side of the bridges I still haven't encountered, and that apparently I'm not yet ready to cross. It's time to cross the neighborhoods in silence, to walk out on tiptoes from 31 rue de Fleurus, where my publishing house resides, right next to where Gertrude Stein lived for years, pick up the pace to reach the river, board a drunken boat for a quiet dinner at dusk, and move, move in circles, as if waiting for someone who's not quite ready to dwell in my ship. For now, I persist, I wait, because waiting has been and is my great talent. There's no one like me to incubate patience within four walls on an abandoned island.

Tomorrow, while we walk the red carpet, my new book, *The Warrior's Daughter*, will be launched in Barcelona and Paris; it's my new novel, full of secrets, clues, and historical twists that unravel the complex path to my father.

I tried to put on the shoes that came with the dress, but they were too small for even my tiny feet. I finally left them behind in the room and came down barefoot. I thought no one would notice because the dress went down to the ground.

Once in the lobby, Gerónimo introduced me to the rest of the team. I hugged Armando, got a thumbs-up for the dress from everyone, but Olatz and Miguel realized immediately that I wasn't wearing shoes. Looking tall while barefoot is not a gift I think I have.

I said something to Gerónimo about the fact that he hadn't

let me see the completed film, and that I'd only been able to view fragments of the documentary parts. He was too nervous to pay attention and just asked me to walk calmly, looking off to infinity and, above all, to not respond to any media questions, and if they insisted or bugged me too much about personal things, he said I should just smile or pull out my phone, indicating I had other priorities. *Why in the devil did he bring me here?* I asked myself, staring him right in the eyes.

"Why can't she respond to questions?" Miguel asked him.

"You're looking very elegant, Miguel," Gerónimo responded, avoiding his question.

Armando was silent but clearly had a million concerns. Just then Olatz came back with new shoes in hand.

There were camera flashes and screams directed at the stars presenting their movies. Everyone was there, and when I say everyone it's because it's not even worth naming them all. It was the precise moment to realize that in a sea of stars and celebrities, you simply don't exist. A name can replace another, a photo can replace another, but by the end of the night, there's just a pastiche of memories that confuses you and hinders your mind.

I walked the red carpet quickly, holding hands with my friends, who protected me from whatever virus or aggression was out there. I walked the red carpet like somebody on a tightrope fifty-five stories high.

"Move along, Gerónimo's here," Lidia kept shouting at us, rushing us along.

I walked the red carpet and it was as if nothing had happened.

★

I walked straight into the theater, with Olatz's incredibly tall shoes on my feet. I glanced at the rear windows, looked for my name on the seats and, what a surprise, I'd been seated right next to Gerónimo. He really did want to legitimize his story with my presence. I smelled his scent; this time it was the same cologne he'd used in Havana. I had a knot in my throat, and from then on decided to just feel rather than look.

Gerónimo stepped up on the stage with his team. For whatever reason, he left me behind; he didn't ask me up with them. Miguel, Armando, Olatz, and I looked at each other. Why? Well, maybe it was because I'm not an actor, nor a producer, nor a photographer. Whatever. Everybody gave a little speech. They spoke in English, of course. There was applause, shouting, whistles.

The lights immediately went down. The actor returned to my side. My friends were behind me, touching my shoulder, letting me know they were there, sending signs of love and moral support. The movie didn't strike me as good or bad. It was a strange film, too long perhaps, saturated with speculation that he tried to save via fictionalizing. Gerónimo has always been an excellent actor. When I saw the images of my house, I thought of Márgara, who came out of the kitchen like a ghost, very quiet, as I looked over photos of my father. When did he take these pictures? I don't remember. Seeing Márgara there in Cannes made me remember all we've gone through together, and what awaits us when I decide to go home.

Gerónimo came into the frame. I saw him move with the lightness of the man I'd fallen in love with, who got me involved in this project and led me to accept who I am, and where I really come from. I quickly understood these images had come from the cameras set up to spy on us. The angles coincided, the grain and consistency of the images were the same as those the officers would play for me during the long raids and invasive interrogations. How did he get them?

Two tears dropped on my hands and my sobs awakened Gerónimo's compassion. Employing the same tone he used just before he left Cuba, he hugged me anxiously and told me he couldn't forget me. I hate compassion, both the word and gesture. I didn't believe a word he said now because he was under the powerful spell of his first public presentation as a director.

I saw my family photos gradually go by, of both the known and the unknown. I confirmed that all the information I'd used in my book was correct, and also that my older brother had died of an overdose in Miami. It was a very sad story and the film was increasingly disjointed. When I focused on the screen a few seconds before the credits, I saw an announcement in English and Spanish: *This film is a work of fiction, and is not inspired by actual events.*

"What do you mean it's not inspired by actual events?" I asked Gerónimo, indignant, while the credits were reflected on my face along with my father's face. The audience burst into a roaring applause.

"Be quiet, please, we'll talk later," Gerónimo said in a very low voice, smiling, well aware the cameras could find him in the darkness.

I rushed out of the theater, running with the shoes in my hand, terrified, and I didn't stop until I'd reached the hotel. I thought I saw Sting when I left, but stopping to say hello was as ridiculous as standing next to Gerónimo supporting his "fiction." I left Miguel and Olatz behind, not counting on them right then. Who remembers a woman as absurd as me who gets mixed up in things like this? I finally reached my room and, without undressing, headed straight for the comfort of a cold shower, which washed away my makeup and the voluminous dress that now seemed so silly. I threw up what little I'd eaten that day.

After a few minutes, I heard Gerónimo's voice from outside the room, asking me to open the door.

I didn't leave the bathroom but he somehow managed to get somebody to let him in; after all, it was his production company that had paid for the room. He came in quietly and sat down on the toilet to explain things to me, impassively, not at all nervous, without any reaction to the spectacle he had before him, just barely acknowledging me under the furious shower that was melting me away.

He arrived full of his success. He'd come only to defend himself, to wipe his image clean, and to make sure I'd shut up so everything would remain between us. Beyond the pain I felt at being manipulated by someone who'd convinced me to confront the truth, there was the matter of his demeanor.

He talked to me as if I were a little girl who can't accept her parents' divorce, or an unstable mental patient who needs to take her meds to calm down. He was very smooth as he explained the inexplicable, what he couldn't take responsibility for even as he said he did. Even after everything we'd gone through together in Havana, he justified the censorship.

According to what he said, it was the State Department who told him the files weren't completely declassified, and that most of the information used to make the film came from unreliable sources. It's going to take more than a decade to verify everything, it's true, because the documents won't be released until Cuba and the United States come to an agreement and take care of the details, which are connected to very delicate matters still to be confirmed. The film's final frame was the only way he could protect himself. According to some biographers, my father had been implicated in the assassination of John F. Kennedy and, as everyone knows, that's another matter that's not entirely open to the public.

I didn't believe a single word he said. Who could believe him after such a series of betrayals?

Armando came to my room, took off my wet dress, and asked Gerónimo to leave. We packed our bags and ran together from that place, full of photographers listening to a story that didn't seem altogether true to them either.

22

From up here, Cuba looks tiny.

So many sagas from this land where water threatens to end it all and leave us talking to ourselves.

The waves weave into the shore, as if the sea is trying to drown the country; but there are limits, and the water always returns to its levels.

Today is Sunday. There's nothing more depressing in Cuba than a Sunday at seven in the evening. Sundays depress me and it's almost seven, the sun is setting and the salt-filtered light pierces the plane's windows.

I know sometimes life down there is infernal. But isn't this my inferno? Here I go, swooping in, landing on what's mine, the things I need to recover.

Here is where I go to search for myself, here is where I belong. This is my scent, this is my light.

I'm lost and I've come back to find myself.

When the plane doors opened, I heard a voice calling out my first and last names. The French flight attendant kindly asked me to please remain in my seat and not leave the plane. I did as she requested. As soon as the last passenger had stepped off, a corps of uniformed and uninformed officers marched in. One of them informed me I could not enter Cuba, that my entry permit had been canceled.

I would wait there, calmly, as the plane was cleaned, refueled, and the new passengers came aboard, and in nine hours, I'd be back in Paris.

But I had no one in Paris. Why should I go back there? My home is here, my only home. Cuba is my family. Cuba is my home. I have no other place to go back to.

I asked several times why my entry was canceled and each time I was told I didn't meet the migratory requirements to return.

I flipped through my passport with them and everything appeared to be in order. They checked my plane ticket for the number of bags and ordered that they be rerouted to my new flight.

They suggested I go to the Cuban Embassy in France to initiate a new process and an investigation to clear up the matter. I reminded them I was on Cuban soil, that I was a Cuban citizen and I had rights . . . "Rights?" asked one of the officers, staring me in the eye.

They suggested I keep my composure and left a young man, armed, to watch over me. He held my passport until the new passengers came onboard. Then he gave it to the chief flight attendant to give back to me when we arrived in France.

A military officer kept guard on the plane until they closed the doors.

The crew transferred me to first class and one of the flight attendants brought me a cup of tea.

I had a claustrophobic panic attack. My country is right

there, just outside. I need to run and take refuge in my house, but they won't let me. This is a nightmare.

We take off. Little by little, I feel Cuba leave my body. My soul tries to stay connected to the earth but it abandons me, detaches from me. In the air, I can't breathe, I'm choking. Little by little, I scatter, I turn to water and salt.

Without Cuba, I don't exist.

I am my island.

CLEO'S POEMS

EXCESS BAGGAGE

If they let me take everything I miss
If they let me take the island and the miracle
I'd have no place to return.
I wouldn't come back to myself
or to memories of you.

POEMS IN CHINESE

I rise every morning before anyone in the village
just to open the cage for the birds that you later hear sing
The night swallows them and silences with black velvet
it betrays you and I awake broken
opening cages swallowing tears
exhaling the remains of my dead wings into the dawn

My eyebrows were tattooed in Chinese and in a delicate
    fashion
Summer in the Orient belongs to that harsh dynastic
    and dry dense pleasure

passions that explode in the dazzling light poisonous
    and blind
I hold on to my distorted inheritance trail of brief erotic
    sketches
lacey breasts
I fleetingly return there to my Asiatic poverties of rice
    and Indian ink
intimate sex
Women moan with desire
I call out your name in pain.

You know my dead and my gestures and my prayers to
    those dead whom
    you call by name
You offer them food and you serve my squalid body
that doesn't swallow that doesn't drink that doesn't
    sleep that hasn't lived here for
centuries
You name the bird and determine if it is free or a
    prisoner by its trill
It is I who lives inside the heart of the bird
She who eats and drinks like the bird is the woman you
    touch and bless

Don't free me from the ritual that feeds your dead
and keeps me alive.

AUTOFICTION

Everything is apocryphal, my life is autofiction, and if I
    write poetry, I return to the original idea
    . . . Certain nights when I'm asleep, the child I was
    returns, that girl I remember who hides
    under my skirt without a handler or a straitjacket.

Everything is apocryphal and I'm a character in an
    unfilmed movie, a version of my
    wishes that doesn't even have my name.

A CAGE WITHIN

And she who is I wants to open the cage
cage that separates me from the living
But we were already   yes   a bit dead what
    with everything and birds hungry for light
Dead from all the words silenced in the
    darkness   you have reached us
Ready to predict from the learned confinement
I strive to translate with vigor my letters engraved on
    the body.

TOY CAGE

I see the traps along the way
but they look like flowers compasses or mirrors
The collection of cages I inherited from my mother
    made me female
I fell as low as the deep sound of my orchestra
That's where I'm going arrogant and enslaved
The onslaught promises the worst

Girl   toy cage
My virgin heart flushed   doesn't
    inherit insult or pain
And it's just that there are no cages inside the body
    of a girl.

A HOUSE WITHIN

There is no possible hiding place here
vanity or mirror
clear translucent structure
clean and deserted
on a small scale

A HOUSE WITHIN
of an uncomfortable rationalism
Japanese equilibrium of broken silk
unjust and icy outcome
without altars or flowers without photos without
    family
passing through and insomnia
patrimony and artifice

A HOUSE WITHIN
No one has gathered here
Not children Nor men Nor ideas.

BRIEF BIOGRAPHY OF RICE

Orphan
born and raised in Saigon
I've paid my way since childhood

Indigo keeps the heart of the lotus white
In certain photos I look like a western girl
they interrogate me when I row in the mangroves and
    sing the truths
My job is to separate the jasmine from the rice
my hobby is to draw you in silence
to erase the excess clothing on your body
You live naked in my silk diary
I follow the line with a raised hand I tear up my figure
    and dislodge you
All I have learned about bombs is read in the past
I'm old to be adopted and young to be crazy
    I go on groping
I know my penance kneeling and mute
thick silence unknown and profitable
I cross vain words on my bicycle
my pedals are silver switchblades breaking the sound
The trail of rice marks the brief path I follow every day
I'm coming to take care of Saigon.

PLAYING HIDE AND SEEK

With my face buried in my arm without cheating
    with my back facing out
leaning against a tree I counted to infinity while they
    hid
one one thousand two one thousand and when I
    opened my sheds nighttime
Where is everyone? So much time spent looking for
    them
One two three four five six seven eight nine ten

How far away   how alone   how lost
   in the courtyard of my own game.

PROMENADE THROUGH PERSONAL MUSEUM

When I abandon, when I take leave, when I let myself
let go of myself
forever
a lock of my hair remains tethered to the past
caught on the wired fence of a minefield
I isolate and punish myself
blood on the mirrors a braid of nightmares and violent
violated mysteries
windows that make me desperately want to flee, nailing
the danger to my feet
forever
a man lies in wait for me between his screams I plead
on my knees the
lost
blueprint
cloistered with names I begin to recognize
methylene blue, orange towns, purges, and rain of
pain
what was the first home with the beating, there was
   a home
there was rest
from this deep dread
when I abandon there are drawers filled with
   sand left behind
butterfly dust on the bed
gold in my hands

emptiness in my eyes
from stretcher to stretcher trying to get
nowhere
fever the queen's body will be cremated
because exposed
she causes shame.

MASAI SPEAR

for José Bedia
They say that what's important about the spear is its
    trajectory
Your destiny depends on that trajectory
It's already flown over your lighted head
It crowns your journey and threads through every
    attempt at flight
In the air, it embodies protection from danger, for your
    home
and howls with an unforgettable blind nighttime whistle
It's the trajectory that's important as it spins so feminine
    and sure
until it hits the wound
Oh the wound, it had been opened long before
someone polished a delirious spearpoint for the rescue.

Many years before it was a spear it was a tree and it's
    now air
and blood and sacred dance magical protection
shelter and faith
Long before it was captured and collected it was rage
poison and antidote

Long before it was jerked from the body it was itself
a body that could accompany us
Long before it was yours it was you yourself pouring
    your body
into another thirst dispersion your soul into other
imprisoned souls
Awakening the dangers from which it always protects
    you
and triumphs
I am and have been your Masai spear your silk blade
    your
offering
Weapon and shelter   in an elevated contact with the
    sun   an arrow sketched
into the moon's secret
A female spear that guards your trajectory with hers
Guarding the sixth senses and the songs of the flesh
The one who will die to come to the rescue
The one who escapes with the prey though it belongs
    to the hunter
I arch on your back I'm the returning desire
I fit in you with or without pain
I'm your eyes which no longer see the distances
Light, airy and mute I silently follow your steps
Immersed in the dampness of another battle I write verses
in air
Trot along the step of the warrior you are and have been
I'm your Masai spear
I've trained alone in infidel combat
In the army of the epic cities

In the jungle that doesn't know humankind
In the abstract crusade of your head when you smoke
    and look at the waters
I'm the warrior's weapon that comes back intact with
    the lion's mane
in my hands
I'm the heart that beats outside the body
I'm your Masai spear
The day I don't return joined to your body resting
on your back
Vigilant and haughty
means I've saved you
Don't be afraid
I only am and have been your Maasai spear.

ESKIMO PROMISE

For you, I'll leave the snow and ski on sand
I won't write graffiti on ice
I'll have a Western accent and summer clothes
my teeth will not soften any flesh but yours
my scent will disappear into your clean lavender
and like the sturgeon drops her caviar I'll drop my name
I'll forget the ritual of the igloo the woman and the
    captive
I'll look at the melting ice as if it were water from my sex
I won't give away what's yours to strangers at the end
    of the night
I'll stay in your bed dodging the fire
I'll erase both bait and fish from my mouth
I'll free the dogs from the sled

I'll try to forget the banishment from ice
we'll winter together while winter pains us
over the edge of the iceberg, traveling on the white isle
there's a frozen tear from my mother
and your father's pleading whisper
perhaps amnesia would be better
though everything may seem from another world
we'll hunt together
it's an Eskimo promise.

A Note About the Author

Wendy Guerra was born in Havana, Cuba, where she was an actress, radio and television host, and protégé of Gabriel García Márquez. After winning the prestigious Bruguera Novel Prize in 2006, she came under surveillance by Cuban intelligence and was removed from her television job. Guerra's work has been widely praised abroad, published in over a dozen languages, yet remains largely unavailable in Cuba, where she still lives. This is her fifth novel, and the second to be translated into English.